A Touch of Texas Irish

by

Linda LaRoque

A Touch of Texas Irish

Cover Art by *Diana Carlile*

The Wild Rose Press, Inc.
PO Box 708
Adams Basin, NY 14410-0708
Visit us at www.thewildrosepress.com

Publishing History
First Cactus Rose Edition, 2017
Print ISBN 978-1-5092-1192-0
Digital ISBN 978-1-5092-1193-7

Published in the United States of America

Acknowledgements

My husband and I were fortunate enough to tour part of Ireland a few years ago. One of my favorite stops was Kinsale, an Irish shipping port and town known for its boating activities, rich history, and fine dining. I hope to be able to visit again one day.

The idea for *A Touch of Texas Irish* was born there. Kinsale had its share of immigrant ships, but not as numerous as the other ports. Many of the ships departing Kinsale traveled to Boston, a city of Protestants where Catholics weren't welcome. What a setting for stories—both nonfiction and fiction. The possibilities are limitless.

~~

Books
Daggett, Marsha. 1984. *Pecos County History: Vol 1,* Midland, Texas: Staked Plains Press.

Websites
"How fast could you travel across the U.S. in the 1800s?" www.mnn.com/greentech/transportation/ stories/ how-fast-could-you-travel-across-the-us-in-the1800s

"Irish Immigrants in America during the 19th Century" www.kinsella.org/history/histira.htm

"The Irish in America: 1840's-1930's" http://xroads.virginia.edu/~ug03/omara-alwala/ irishkennedys.html

"OLD WEST LEGENDS Stagecoach Terms and Slang" http://www.legendsofamerica.com/we-stagecoachterms.html

"Passenger Trains Accelerate and Reduce Cost of Travel" www.railswest.com/passengertrains.html

"Property Rights of Women in Nineteenth-Century England"
http://www.123helpme.com/view.asp?id=18566

"Pullman Sleeping Cars add Comfort to Overnight Travel" www.railswest.com/pullman.html

"Railroads" https://tshaonline.org/handbook/online/articles/eqr01

"San Antonio Transportation History Ox, Mule, and Horse Drawn Era 1845-1910" http://www.txtransportationmuseum.org/history-ox-mule-horse.php

"Stagecoaching in Texas" www.texasalmanac.com/topics/history/stagecoaching-texas

"The Stagecoaches" www.tombstonetimes.com/stories/stagecoaches.html

~*~

Other Books by Linda LaRoque
available at The Wild Rose Press, Inc.

A Stolen Chance
Desires of the Heart
My Heart Will Find Yours
Flames on the Sky

~*~

…and the trilogy titled *A Time of Their Own*
which includes
A Law of Her Own
A Marshal of Her Own
A Love of His Own

Chapter One

Mitchelstown, County Cork, Ireland, January 1890

Aileen sat beside the bed, her book of poems forgotten in her lap. She listened for every breath, fearing it would be Mam's last—Maureen Callahan Lynch, the beautiful and vibrant woman who had loved and guided Aileen for the whole eighteen years of her life. Her striking chestnut hair, now streaked with gray, spread across the pillow. The doctor called her illness cancer—a growth on her lungs ate away at her health, bit by bit. Soon it would claim her life.

Aileen leaned toward the bed. She ran her fingers through the long tresses of Mam's hair. As a child, she had often brushed the glorious auburn locks. It would crackle with life at each stroke of the brush—now the dry strands easily broke, leaving remnants on the linens. "Oh, Mam, I don't want you to go. I'm going to miss you so...so much." She dropped her head to the mattress and wept.

"My girl, don't take on so. I'm ready to leave this earth and feel whole again." Mam caressed the top of Aileen's head. "I want you to live and enjoy your youth. You've spent too much time in this sickroom taking care of me." A thump resounded on her forehead. Startled, Aileen giggled as she rubbed the offended spot. Mam used to bop her if her attention wandered as a girl. "That's what I want to hear—laughter. Don't wallow in your grief." With the corner of the sheet, she wiped the moisture from Aileen's cheeks. "Let me go, my darling girl."

Aileen's throat and chest ached. She tried to hold her tears back, but she had to release them or choke. She wailed, "You...you've been the best...Mam... Mam...a girl could have." She sniffed, pulled the kerchief from her waistband, and blew her nose. "I...I love you, but I'll try to do as you ask."

"That's my girl. Now you go have tea and send your da up to keep me company for awhile."

She stood and kissed her mother's cheek, the paper-thin skin cold to the touch. "Yes, ma'am. I will."

An hour later, Da entered the parlor. His shoulders sagged, and he steadied himself with the doorframe. "She's passed. Your mother...is gone." His voice choked on the words and turned to sobs. He held out his arms.

"Oh, Da." Aileen walked into his embrace, and they wept together. "Mam was ready. For us to hope she could live longer would be selfish, don't you think?"

He stepped back and wiped his tears with his handkerchief. "Aye, I do. She hurt so much. Now the pain is gone."

"Sit down, and I'll pour you a cup of tea." They sat quietly side by side on the sofa. The burial arrangements were made. The housemaids, Lucy and Mabel, came in and draped the window and mirror in black crape. Aileen suspected the mourning wreath adorned their front door.

Two hours later, Aileen and their housekeeper,

Mattie, had her mother washed and dressed for viewing. The undertaker and his assistant arrived from the village with the casket. A table, to hold the coffin, was brought from the library and stood alone at one end of the parlor.

Aileen arranged her mother's clothes, folded her hands over her small Bible, and added finishing touches to her hair. Maureen Callahan Lynch was as regal in death as she had been in life. The lines of pain were gone. A tilt of her lips gave the suggestion of a smile.

"Rest in peace, Mam."

****

The wake began immediately. The funeral would take place the next morning. News traveled to Mitchelstown and the surrounding area. Friends and neighbors arrived in small groups to pay their respects. Mam had no family. Aileen had never learned the details of her family history, simply that her mother was an only child. Mam's mother was deceased, and she and her father were estranged. Now she wished she'd asked more questions.

Dressed in a black paramatta silk dress with a crimped crape collar, she was in full mourning. She'd pulled her auburn hair back into a ball and held it in place with a snood. Aileen alternated between sitting in a chair at one end of the casket and standing with their guests. Father, in his finest dark suit, stood with her, coming to her side often. Mam was a well-loved member of their community. She had given generously of her time, when her health permitted, and her money to help the less fortunate. The room filled with flowers, their sweet scent creating a strong aroma masking the smell of death.

Mattie, Lucy, and Mabel kept food on the table in the dining room for guests to take refreshment. Their butler, Charles, stayed busy showing people in and out of the house. By dusk, Aileen could no longer stand. Fortunately, all the visitors had left.

At last she could stretch out on the sofa for a short respite. She had sent Charles off to rest earlier. Being elderly, he was worn out by the steady traffic. Hopefully they'd have no more visitors tonight.

****

Aileen smoothed the skirt of her dress before knocking on the door of her father's office. Since her mother's passing yesterday morning, and her interment today, she'd not had a moment to rest and had eaten very little. Her stomach grumbled in protest. Lightheaded for a moment, she swayed and caught hold of the doorframe to keep from stumbling.

Inhaling deeply, she knocked on the ten-foot mahogany door. A gruff "Enter" resonated from inside. She exhaled, turned the knob, and entered the room. Their lawyer, Mr. Jamison, sat at her father's large desk, which monopolized the middle of the room. Father rose from the brown leather sofa opposite the wall of books and took her hand. "Are you up to this, daughter?"

She tried to smile, but feared her expression resembled a grimace, and nodded. "Let's get it over with, Father." He led her to a seat on the couch.

Mr. Jamison peered over his spectacles and asked, "Is this everyone, Mr. Lynch?"

Father glanced around the room to see all were assembled—the butler, the housekeeper/cook, two housemaids, and the groom.

"Yes." He joined her on the sofa. "You may begin."

Mr. Jamison cleared his throat, adjusted his eyeglasses, and read aloud.

"I, Maureen Callahan Lynch, being of sound mind and body on this day May 1, 1889, designate this document to be my last will and testament. It is my wish neither this house nor any member of my family continue mourning customs after the six-week period."

Stunned, Aileen glanced at her father for answers. With palms up, he shrugged. Whispers buzzed among the staff. Mattie visibly smiled and nodded.

"I hereby bequeath to my loyal butler Charles Hathaway, and to my housekeeper and cook Mattie Walsh, thirty pounds a year each, for the remainder of their lives."

Mattie burst into tears. Charles patted her shoulder but appeared to be as moved as Mattie. The list continued with each of the staff, those young enough to seek employment elsewhere receiving a sum of ten pounds to tide them over until they found other work.

Mr. Jamison stood and handed every young staff member an envelope. "You'll find your ten pounds inside, with a letter of reference. Mrs. Lynch did ask that you stay on until either Miss or Mr. Lynch decide to move elsewhere." He also nodded to Charles and Mattie.

"Yes, sir."

"Of course, sir."

"Mr. Hathaway and Mrs. Walsh, your envelopes contain the first year of your pension, with a personal note. You'll receive the next installment each year at this time after your retirement."

Aileen's spirit lifted at the joy on the staff's faces. "Now then, if you will leave us, the remainder of the reading is to be private." They all stood and exited the room, the older ones silent and the younger speaking in whispered tones. She glanced at her father. His face was pale and sweat lined his brow.

"Father, are you all right?"

He patted her hand. "I'm fine. Just ready for this to be over."

She laced her hand under his arm and hugged him. "Me too, Da. Me too."

Mr. Jamison returned to the desk, lifted the papers, and continued reading. *"To my husband, Quinton Lynch, I leave one hundred fifty pounds a year for life, and the option to remain in this house for the remainder of his life or until he remarries. This home, its contents, and all my remaining worldly goods and assets I leave to my daughter, Aileen Callahan Lynch. Mr. Jamison will manage her estate until such time as she marries or upon her death. If she dies without issue, what remains of her estate is to be divided among the following charities."* He read a long list, names which meant nothing to Aileen.

Her father dropped his head back against the sofa. Pulling on the tight collar of his shirt, he gasped for air.

"Da, what's wrong?" Aileen worked to loosen his cravat, while Mr. Jamison poured him a glass of water and handed him the glass. Fearing he'd drop it, Aileen held the tumbler steady as he drank.

"Perhaps a touch of brandy instead."

He sipped the water and pushed the tumbler away. "No, no brandy. I think I'm all right now." He sat up straighter. "Go ahead with the reading."

"This concludes the will in its entirety. All that is left is for you both to sign all four copies of the will, indicating you understand the conditions." He spread papers out on the desk. Father pushed himself up and off the sofa. When she tried to help, he held a hand up, refusing her aid.

"I'm fine." He walked to the desk and perused each document before reaching for the pen. The bold strokes of the nib scratching across the paper echoed around the room. Finished, he set the pen aside and turned. "I think I'll lie down for a while." He shook Mr. Jamison's hand. "Thank you for staying so late. We'd be pleased if you'd join us for dinner and stay the night. Dublin is a long drive from here, and the drive can be dangerous at this hour."

Aileen approached the window, held the black drape back to gaze through the windowpanes. Dusk was fast approaching.

"Thank you for your hospitality, Mr. Lynch. It has been a long and tiring day, more so for you and Miss Lynch than myself. If you're sure I'm not a bother, I'd be pleased to stay."

"No trouble at all, Mr. Jamison." He turned to Aileen and kissed her cheek. "Daughter, I believe I'll eat in my room tonight. Please tell Mattie."

"Yes, Da. I will." She watched as he left the room, closing the door behind him. He appeared to have aged in the past hour. Mother's will had evidently been as much a shock for him as for her. "Mr. Jamison, can you tell me why Mother left so much to me and so little to my father?" The difference didn't make sense. Could it be a mistake?

He held out the pen to her. "Yes, I will, but first

please sign these documents so I can put them away."

Aileen did as the lawyer asked, and he placed the papers in four stacks. "One copy is for your father and one for you. Of the other two, one will be filed at my office and one at the courthouse of Cork County."

He sat down behind the desk and motioned for her to take a seat also. She perched on the edge of one of the chairs vacated by the staff.

"I don't know if you're aware, but the wealth in your family was your mother's. Mrs. Lynch inherited it from your deceased grandmother." He folded his hands on the desktop. "I hate to be the one to tell you this, Miss Lynch, but your father has gambled away a good amount of the estate's assets. Your mother was afraid you'd be left a pauper. She couldn't let that happen."

Unable to speak, Aileen stared at the man. "I...I had no idea. Why didn't Mother tell me?" She lifted a handkerchief from her pocket and twisted the fabric in her hand. It was a bad habit, one she resorted to when upset or nervous. Mam had chided her for the practice often. Had her mother been worried about money before her death? If so, yes, Aileen's future would be a top concern.

"I'm sure your mother didn't want to worry you, or for you to think badly of your father."

Aileen stood and paced the room, as if each step would bring her closer to understanding how her father's gambling had gone unnoticed. Most of their thoroughbred horses were missing from the stable. Why had she not questioned her father? His horse, her mare, and the carriage horses were still in the building, so it had never occurred to her to ask.

"Miss Lynch, I must inform you that you'll not be

allowed to give or loan any monies to your father as long as I'm in charge of your funds." She plopped down on the sofa. At least that was one issue she wouldn't have to discuss with Father. "This must sound harsh, but your mother didn't want to put your home at risk of being repossessed and liquidated to pay his debts."

"How could I have been so blind?"

"Don't chide yourself. Individuals who gamble habitually are good at hiding that habit from their loved ones. I've seen it over and over again." He gathered his papers and those to be filed in the courthouse and slipped both batches into his satchel. The others he left in two piles on the desk. "Can I help you with anything else?"

"No, sir. Thank you. I believe it will take some time to absorb all of this information."

He nodded. "Of course, but please understand this: your mother trusted me. I hope you will also. If anything comes up about the will or money, anything you don't understand or need help with, contact me. The stable lad carried missives for your mother when needed. I'm sure the boy will do the same for you."

"I'll do that, and thank you."

"You're most welcome." He stood. "I'd like to retire now, if you have no further questions."

"Of course. I'll show you to your room." Aileen stood. Her head spun. She reached out to steady herself on the corner of the desk.

"Miss Lynch..." He rushed to help her sit back down. "Let me call Mr. Hathaway and Mrs. Walsh." Within minutes they were both in the room fussing over her. For once, their coddling was appreciated.

"Charles, show Mr. Jamison to his room. I will send a tray along for him shortly." Mattie took command. She slipped an arm around Aileen's waist and helped her stand. "Come along, dearie. You need to have some food in your stomach and be tucked into bed."

Sometime later, Aileen was propped up in bed in a warm nightgown. Mattie sat beside her, spooning a rich cream of chicken soup into her mouth. "Mmm, it's delicious, Mattie. I don't believe I've ever tasted better."

Mattie chuckled. "'Spect it's because you're so hungry."

Aileen clutched the older woman's hand. "I love you, Mattie."

"I know you do, lass, and I you…like you're me own wee bairn." She set the bowl aside and tucked the covers in around Aileen. "Now you get a good night's rest. The world will be a little brighter tomorrow."

Chapter Two

"Good morning, miss." Mabel piled pillows behind Aileen's head and back and then set the breakfast tray on the bed. "All your favorites. Cook hopes your appetite is better this morning." From the hearty display before her, Aileen could want for nothing—crisp bacon, scones, clotted cream and strawberries, and a pot of her favorite breakfast tea.

"Thank you, Mabel. Tell Cook she's outdone herself."

"Would you like me to draw you a warm bath while you're eating?"

"That would be lovely, but today only. I know you have other duties, and I don't need to be coddled. I can fend for myself." Her throat closed, and she struggled not to cry. Her mother had insisted Aileen not be dependent on a maid. She'd grown up dressing herself. "But I do thank ye all for your devotion."

Mabel appeared about to cry herself. She bobbed a curtsey and strode to the door to the bathing room. Aileen bit into the still warm orange scone and heard water filling the tub as she chewed. Mabel arrived back at Aileen's bedside. "I forgot something, miss." She took an envelope from her apron pocket and handed her a letter. "Mr. Jamison asked me to give this to you soon as you woke."

Aileen licked sugar from her fingers and opened

11

the envelope.

Miss Lynch,

Remember what I said: if ever in need of my assistance, you need only send a message. Either one of my associates or I will contact you straight away.

Albert Jamison

It was nice to have someone other than her father to lean on. The news of his gambling had been a blow. She knew he played cards at his club in Dublin, but he wasn't gone very often, especially after Mam's illness turned bad. He'd been by her bedside as often as possible. Of course, the woolen mill took much of his time, but perhaps he'd slipped away from work to visit the city.

Up and dressed, she descended the stairs to plan the week's menu with Cook. She'd taken over her mother's duties after illness caused her to be bedridden. Near the foot of the stairs, loud voices from the office halted her descent. *What on earth...?* A crash rattled the painting on the wall and sent her down the remaining stairs and barging into the room.

"Father?" At the sound of her voice, both men, her father and a gentleman unknown to her, broke apart. Father stumbled, knocked the small pie-top table over on its side, with one leg askew, and landed on his bum. He scrambled up from the floor as the large younger man tried to right the table. The lamp lay shattered on the wool rug.

"What's going on?"

"Just got our feet tangled, and I ended up in a heap." He straightened his clothes and held his hands out to show he was unharmed.

"You're sure you're not hurt?"

"I'm fine." He glanced at the lopsided table and shook his head. "Though it seems your mother's fine table needs some repair."

"I'll leave you, then, and send Lucy to clean up the oil on the rug. We don't need a fire."

"Thank you, Aileen."

"Can I bring you tea?"

"No, dear. Mr. MacAuley was just leaving."

Staring openly at her, the man opened his mouth as if to dispute Da's words. Da silenced him with a glare. Their guest merely nodded and returned his attention to her father.

"All right, then." She left the room, closing the door behind her. Something wasn't right here. She suspected the story about tangled feet was a lie.

****

"You might have told me you had such a delightful daughter, Lynch. I find your unwillingness to introduce us a slight on your part." They occupied a booth in a darkened corner of the nondescript tavern. Under normal circumstances, neither one of them would be seen frequenting such a scurvy place.

Quinton chided himself, again, for his mistake in inviting Brian MacAuley into their home the previous day. The man preyed on people with weaknesses…like himself. He rued the day he'd met the man. For several months there, the man had fooled Quinton. He'd thought him the cock of the walk, throwing lavish card parties in his extravagant home in Dublin. Of course alcohol ran freely, and MacAuley's guests liberally imbibed. Then, when the man had his claws in a soul, he started ripping away the flesh, one layer at a time. Just last month, one of the man's victims took his own life after losing his funds and his home. His wife and children were forced to retire to the country to live with her parents.

Now he'd turned his attention to Quinton, who struggled to prevent a shiver of revulsion from shaking his frame. The thought of Brian MacAuley showing interest in Aileen appalled him. He must keep that monster away from her. "There is no need for you to become acquainted with my daughter. Stay away from her and my home."

"Your thirty days will be up next week, Lynch. You assured me you'd come into a sum of money when your wife passed away. Well, I waited. Now I want my money."

"There is a problem." Quinton removed his handkerchief from inside his jacket pocket and mopped his brow. "My wife learned of my gambling, of the missing heirlooms, and the absent thoroughbred horses." He cleared his throat. "She left everything to our daughter."

"Well, get it from her, man."

"I can't. Our lawyer is in control of her assets, and I can assure you he'll not give me a pence of my daughter's inheritance."

Brian studied his fingernails and flashed a smile that didn't quite reach his eyes. "Well, then, it seems I'll be courting Miss Lynch."

"You'll do no such thing."

MacAuley grabbed Quinton's arm. His pale blue gaze turned ice cold and bore into Quinton's. "You listen to me. One week and I'll come calling. You talk your daughter into finding a way to get the money, or have her prepared to receive me as a suitor. If no money, I'll take the daughter." He shoved Quinton. His chair skittered backward. "Money or your daughter." He smirked. "I'll be calling soon to get an answer."

****

Father laid his newspaper to the side of his breakfast plate. "It's a lovely day. What are your plans?"

"I want to go through more of Mam's things, get her clothes ready to give to the church." She shook her head. "'Tis a tedious and emotional chore." So many of Mam's dresses brought back fond memories. Few could be saved, but some of the black, gray, and lavender dresses could be altered for Aileen's year of mourning. She couldn't convince herself to limit her show of respect to six weeks.

"Why don't you set aside time to take tea with me and a guest this afternoon?"

"I don't really feel like entertaining, and with it being so close to Mam's passing, it is not really proper."

"It's not socializing but tea with a friend who'd like to extend his condolences. He wants to see how we're doing, if he can help us in any way." He stood, strode to the sideboard, and returned to the table with the coffee carafe. After pouring himself a cup, he returned it to the buffet counter. "I'd like you to meet him and pour for us." Lifting his cup, he peered at her over the rising steam. "Plus, he wants to apologize to you for our roughhousing the other morning."

"He's the man you tussled with in the study?"

"Yes, he is, but—"

"Why would you want me to meet such a man?"

"You saw him in an unfavorable light, dear. Give

him another chance."

"Why should I? He's nothing to me."

"It would make me feel better. I don't want you thinking unfavorably of my friends and acquaintances."

"All right, Da. But don't expect me to sit around all afternoon and chat about your woolen mill or whatever it is you men talk about. And remember, though Mother said six weeks, my mourning period will last a year."

"Of course I won't forget. I do wish you'd reconsider and abide by your mother's wishes, though." He dropped a kiss on her head. "Thank you, dear. Three o'clock sharp."

****

Aileen didn't know whether to be interested or wary of her father's friend. He was taller than Da, though her sire couldn't be considered more than barely above average in height. Some would consider their visitor's pale features to be handsome, but to Aileen, he appeared on the colorless side. His pale blue eyes instilled distrust. Perhaps her thinking was due to her family's vivid coloring, especially Father's red hair and deep blue eyes. She should meet him with an open mind.

Both men stood when she entered the parlor. "Brian, this is my daughter, Aileen Callahan Lynch. Aileen, Mr. MacAuley is an acquaintance from my club in Dublin. He's in Mitchelstown for a few days on business."

The man took her proffered hand and planted a wet kiss on the back of it. She jerked it from his grasp, disgusted by the intimacy.

"I'm pleased to meet you, Miss Lynch."

"You also, sir." She stepped to the fireplace and

rang for Lucy. "Please have a seat. Our tea should be right along."

On cue, Lucy rolled the teacart in and set it beside Aileen's chair. "Anything else, miss?"

"No, that will be all for now."

Aileen handed each of the men a napkin. "How do you take your tea, Mr. MacAuley?"

"One sugar, no milk." She stirred his tea and handed him his cup, and then offered the plate of pastries to him. He selected two and placed them on his saucer.

She handed Da his tea, and he helped himself to another pastry. "I must tell Mattie these lemon squares are one of her best creations."

"Da, you say that every time Mattie introduces a new pastry." The man did love his sweets. "Best watch your figure. We don't want you going to fat in your old age."

He had tea in his mouth and choked at her words. He glanced down and pulled on his suit vest. "I've owned this waistcoat for years, and it still fits."

MacAuley watched them with a smile on his face. "Miss Lynch, it's delightful to see your playful joking with your da. Not many fathers and daughters are as close." He took the last sip of his tea and placed his cup on a side table. "I must get to the point of why I'm here today." His smile wilted into an expression of contrition. "Miss Lynch, I beg your forgiveness for my rowdiness while in your home the other evening."

Aileen glanced at her father. He picked lint off his wool trousers and wouldn't make eye contact with her—odd behavior for him.

"Of course, Mr. MacAuley, I forgive you. After all,

you weren't alone in your behavior."

Father cleared his throat. "Yes, I was as much at fault."

"Just what exactly were you doing?"

"Well…uh…" He waved a hand at their guest. "That man challenged me into standing arm wrestling."

She turned her attention to the younger man. He nodded in agreement.

"Why on earth would you participate in such horseplay as this in a house of mourning? Actually, even this visit goes against society's sense of what is proper during this time."

"That's it exactly." Mr. MacAuley leaned forward, his hands on his knees. "Your father was so down, I thought to lighten his mood. My idea was in very poor taste."

"Yes, indeed, sir. It was." She stood, and they joined her. "Please excuse me now. I'd like to return to my room."

The man seized her arm. "Not so fast, young lady. We have something else to discuss."

Father knocked his arm away and stepped between them. "You'll no' be touching me daughter, Brian."

"Of course, what was I thinking? It seems I remember you owe me, old man."

"You'll not be getting it by making free with the lass."

"Of course, of course. I do beg your pardon."

She held his gaze, trying to make up her mind, and then nodded.

"Thank you." He bowed to Aileen. "Miss Lynch, may I call on you?"

She stiffened. "No, sir, you may not." She couldn't

believe her father hadn't stepped in to say something. "First of all, we do not suit. Secondly, I am in mourning and will be for a year." *Why, the nerve of the man!* Back straight, she strode toward the door.

"Quinton, old man. Looks like you'll be going to debtor's prison." He studied his nails. "At least with your yearly allowance you'll be able to pay for one of the better cells and decent food. That won't leave much to save to pay off your debt to me, however."

Aileen turned to her father. Face ashen and shaking, he gripped the back of the sofa to hold himself up. "Is this true, Father?"

He nodded and reached out to her. "I'm so sorry. Please help me. I'd die in prison."

"How much do you owe?"

When her father couldn't get the words out, Mr. MacAuley spoke up for him. "Fifteen hundred pounds."

She sagged into the nearest chair. Mr. Jamison said he'd not give her money for father's debts. What could she do? If she couldn't get the money, Da would go to prison. "Can't you sell the woolen mill? Wouldn't that bring enough to pay this charlatan?"

"Now, now, my dear, no name calling, if you please. I already own half of the mill, my dear, so his half wouldn't be enough."

Father, with his hands over his face, wept openly. His sobs tore at her heart, but she couldn't help him. This mess was of his making. Surely he didn't expect her to be courted by a man who took advantage of his weakness. He coughed to clear his throat. "Can't you get the money from Mr. Jamison? I promise I'll find a way to pay the sum back."

"Mr. Jamison informed me I couldn't loan or give

you any money. It was Mother's wish that my inheritance not be diminished because of your gambling."

He dropped onto the sofa and mopped at his wet face with his handkerchief. "Will you at least try to get the money? I know you don't want me to go to debtor's prison. It would only bring you more shame."

Tears pooled in her eyes and threatened to spill over. Her mother hadn't been in the ground two days, and now they faced this dilemma. She squeezed the bridge of her nose. Her head pounded with each beat of her heart. The lawyer had been quite clear in his instructions, but she could ask. If nothing else, perhaps he could advise her on what to do. Seeing Father go to prison would break her heart. Mother must have been heartsick to see Father's decline in judgment.

Mr. MacAuley smiled, his eyes cold...calculating. "I'll not be waiting long, Miss Lynch. I want me money or your attentions." He smoothed his short, clipped mustache, its fuzz so pale it was scarcely noticeable. "Now, not just your favors. You're a beautiful young woman. I think you'd be an admirable wife for me." He shrugged. "Of course, if you'd rather just be my mistress, we can draw up an agreement which will be satisfactory to both parties."

She could only stare at the odious man. Father's once-pale face bloomed red. He lurched from the sofa with fists knotted and lunged at MacAuley. Laughing, the man stepped aside, and Father missed.

"Now, now, old chap. There is no need to get physical." He adjusted his cravat. "I'll see myself out. One week, and I'll return for your decision...or the money."

The front door slammed. "Daughter, you'd not let me rot away in prison, would you?" His hands shook. "I'd die locked up in a cell."

"What about me? You expect me to marry that man and submit to his attentions...for...for you?" She shuddered. "The thought makes me ill. How can your conscience bear such misuse of me?"

He dropped into a chair, his head in his hands. "I can think of no other way." He raised his head, his gaze pleading. "Please do this for me."

Chapter Three

Mr. Jamison ushered her to a chair in front of his desk and returned to his own. "Can I get you a cup of tea, or perhaps water?"

"No, thank you." She'd not been in his office before, so she glanced around the room at the photographs of his family and the certificates exhibited on the wall.

"Miss Lynch, you should have sent a note. I'd have come to see you immediately."

"I needed to come to town anyway, so the trip was no trouble." She fiddled with the straps of her handbag. Her father's situation wasn't something of which to be proud, and she couldn't seem to find the right words to broach the subject. He already knew her father had a pile of debt, but Aileen hated to waste his time by asking for money he'd previously said she couldn't use on her father.

"What can I do for you today? Do you need money for shopping or household expenses?"

"Mr. Jamison, I'm afraid I'm in a bind." The lawyer listened to her dilemma and patted her shoulder as she cried. "The man is evil. I can't stand the thought of being near him, much less becoming his wife."

His secretary rolled in a tea tray. Older, with graying hair, the middle-aged woman handed Aileen a cup of the refreshing brew. Concern etched her brow.

"No more crying, dearie. A spot of tea will fix you up right and proper."

Aileen took a sip and smiled up at the woman. "It's very good. Thank you."

"You're welcome. It's me own special blend." She nodded to the lawyer. "Now, you put your trust in Mr. Jamison. He'll put everything to rights."

Mr. Jamison tapped his pencil against the note pad in front of him. "There is nothing I can do to keep Mr. MacAuley from sending your father to debtor's prison. Your father cannot force you to marry against your will, and certainly he cannot make you be this man's mistress." This was common knowledge to Aileen, but surely the man could advise her on what to do.

Hands clenched in her lap, she said, "He's coming back in three days for my answer." She'd spent too much time fretting over what to do. Now the time was upon her.

"As I see it, you have three options. Marry the man or become his mistress, neither of which is satisfactory. Or third, let your father go to prison. Though I cannot give you money to loan him, I can give you a stipend each month to pay for his lodging and food while in gaol. That would allow him to save his yearly one hundred fifty pounds to repay Mr. MacAuley. It would take him ten years, but at least you'd not be married to someone you despised." He studied her. "Do you believe your father shallow enough to pressure you into marrying this man or becoming his paramour?"

Her thoughts rocked back and forth between the pleading in his eyes and his fury at Mr. MacAuley's shady proposition. "I don't know. I truly don't. He is torn, for sure."

"Are you strong enough to allow your father to go to debtor's prison? Or would the guilt eat away at you until you gave in to MacAuley's demands?"

She shook her head. "Aye, it would. I'd give in. "

"When you marry, the money reverts to your control. If you decide then to pay your father's debt, you'll be free to do so." He turned his mouth up on one side and shook his head. "Who's to say? He might go right back to gambling, and gambling takes place in jail also.

"There seems to be only one solution for you at this time. We must spirit you away from under your father's nose, so he can't ply you with pressure. He'll serve his time, and I'll see to it that he receives good care at the prison." He arched a slightly graying brow. "Can you accept that alternative?"

"It will hurt, but yes. I have no choice." She willed her bottom lip to keep from trembling.

"Your mother feared this might happen and had me make arrangements just in case. She'd had Mr. MacAuley investigated and suspected he would cause some kind of problem."

Poor Mam. How the situation must have upset her. "Where will I go?"

"To America."

****

Mr. Jamison arrived the following morning. They stood in the kitchen as Aileen prepared to leave and said her goodbyes to the staff. She'd written her father a letter and left it on his desk. "Now, Miss Lynch, we'll meet another carriage just outside Mitchelstown. My niece will be waiting inside the vehicle and will accompany you on your journey." He gestured to her luggage. "Is this all you're carrying with you?"

"Yes, sir. These are just a few essentials for the voyage." She'd packed a large trunk, and Charles would take it to Dublin for shipping overseas.

Mattie patted Aileen's arm. "Your mother asked me to hide several of her family heirlooms to save for you. I put them and a small portrait of your mother and father in the chest Mr. Jamison will ship for you."

"Oh, Mattie." She fell into the cook's arms and wept on her shoulder as she had so many times as a child with a skinned knee or some other little ailment. Cook always had cookies for just such aches and pains. "What will I do without you?"

Mattie drew back and patted her cheek. "You'll live and be happy. That's what your mother wanted. Don't disappoint her or this old woman."

Mabel held Aileen's warmest cloak, and she draped it over Aileen's shoulders. Lucy handed her a bonnet. Aileen set it on her head and tied the ribbon under her chin. The cheerful colors did nothing to lift her spirits. Mattie had convinced her to leave her black clothes behind so she'd blend in with the public. People might remember seeing a young woman in mourning.

She'd worn heavy socks with sturdy boots for the trip. Her slippers were tucked inside her reticule.

Charles stepped up. "Now, lass, you be careful. Don't trust no one, especially when you're near the docks."

"I won't, Charles." She hugged him, and the bent old man patted her shoulder. When he pulled back, his rheumy blue eyes held moisture. Voice gruff, he added, "We'll miss you, but we are grateful to see you out of the clutches of that man." He turned, mumbling something like, "The man should be horse-whipped."

"All right now," said Mr. Jamison. "You all know what to say after we leave?"

They all bobbed their heads, and Mattie remarked, "She left with you, and we weren't told where she was going."

With Aileen's suitcase in his hand, he opened the back door and ushered her out of the kitchen and into the yard. Though the crisp air chilled her nose, the sky was cloudless, and the sun shone down on them. The shamrocks around the garden walk were blooming. She stopped and picked one of the white blooms. A sense of loss filled her. She was leaving everything near and dear to her. Straightening her back, she resolved to return one day.

When they reached Mr. Jamison's carriage, Aileen turned for one last look. Mobley House sat proudly on the terraced landscape. Plants in varying stages of growth added color to the gray stone.

"Come, Miss Aileen. We've no more time to look."

"Where in America am I going, Mr. Jamison?"

"To Boston, Massachusetts."

****

It was almost dark when Quinton Lynch entered the house after a long day at the mill. They were shorthanded at the dyeing vats, putting them behind schedule for their shipment of blankets. One of the carding machines had broken, and men were working overtime tonight to fix it. He stopped at the sideboard in his office and poured a glass of whiskey before slumping in his desk chair. Surely tomorrow would be better.

He took a hefty swig of the alcohol. It burned its

way down to his stomach and eased the knot there. If only Brian MacAuley would get off his back, he might be able to relax. Aileen. His slammed his glass on the desk and dropped his head into his hands. The fear of going to prison turned his insides to water. What kind of father was he to put his daughter anywhere near MacAuley's clutches? But that's exactly what he'd done. He was a coward. The shame of it all... How could he stand himself? He finished the whiskey.

Aileen was a good girl, always thinking of others, obedient. Why, look at how she'd spent hours each day for the past six months caring for her mother. The lass would do what needed to be done to prevent his incarceration and the slander on their family name. Yes, she'd sacrifice her happiness, and he'd wallow in guilt the remainder of his life. Surely she'd marry the man rather than become his mistress. He'd put his foot down on that score.

He made to stand and noticed an envelope propped up in front of the portrait of Maureen and Aileen, on one corner of his desk. It wasn't sealed, so he slipped the sheet of stationary out and unfolded it to see Aileen's signature at the bottom. Chills shot down his spine.

Dear Father,

It breaks my heart to leave you this way, but I can't marry that evil man, even to save you from prison. I'm sorry and pray you'll forgive me.

Mr. Jamison will pay your expenses at the prison, so your yearly allotment can go toward your debt. Perhaps Mr. MacAuley will purchase your half of the mill to lower your debt.

I'm going to America. I will send letters to you via

Mr. Jamison.

> *I love you, Da.*
> *Aileen*

Quinton sat, his eyes focused on the words, his mind on where her decision would leave him...in Bridewell Prison, to rot away and die.

He slammed the letter down and sent the items on his desk, including the miniature portrait, flying across the room to break against the bricks of the fireplace. How dare she treat him this way? After all he'd done for her the past eighteen years. The ungrateful chit. She'd rue her choice, and she'd marry MacAuley if he had to force her at gunpoint.

****

Aileen opened the curtained window to catch a glimpse of the landscape. Soon they'd pass through Kinsale. Though she'd been through the town many times, she'd never seen it in this light...and it was possibly her last time. The quaint seaside town was a favorite vacation spot and famous for its fine food and beautiful scenery. Sadness rushed through her, exposing a bottomless hole in her heart. Tears gathered in her eyes. She swallowed the lump in her throat and brushed aside the moisture on her cheeks. In all probability, she'd never see her homeland again.

Mr. Jamison warned her not to be seen by anyone who might lead her father to her whereabouts. She'd arrive at the ship, board without delay, and stay in her stateroom until they were well out to sea. Mr. Jamison and her mother had made plans for her escape, prepared for an emergency such as this. Poor Mam...burdened with troublesome worries while on her deathbed. The kind solicitor had purchased her ticket more than a month ago—Aileen's father would be searching for a recent booking for a young woman traveling alone.

Lidia Jamison, Mr. Jamison's niece, sat across from Aileen in the carriage, her dark hair pinned up and hidden under a brown felt "Bebe" bonnet. Aileen had seen a picture of one similar in *Ehrich's Fashion Quarterly*, a journal her father had ordered for her. The color of Lidia's hat brought out the deep chestnut of her eyes. "Now, Miss Aileen, best keep your head away from the window. Why, anyone could be out there and catch a peek at you." About her own age, Lidia seemed older, more mature.

She leaned back against the seat. "You don't have to call me 'Miss Aileen.' "

"Yes, miss, I do. Uncle said we must keep this as formal as possible to prevent suspicion. I am your maid, and you're a genteel lady, until we step off the ship in Boston and are in Uncle Avery's custody."

"It's terribly kind of him to take me in and help me get established." Established doing what, Aileen didn't have a clue. She didn't need to work, but at her age she couldn't live alone and didn't want to impose on Mr. Jamison and his wife.

Lidia sniffed. "Kind, nothing. He's being paid generously to take care of you, so don't feel beholden." She shrugged. "I mean, it's nice of them and all, but you don't owe them anything. And you know, most Irish have large families. Uncle has three children, so a couple more people in the house won't be a problem."

Mr. Jamison had said she'd money enough to live comfortably for a long time. He would continue to invest her funds so they would grow, and he'd send her allowance as she needed it, but when she turned twenty-one or married, she'd have free access to the funds.

The carriage wheel hit a hole in the road, and they bounced up and landed off-center on their seats. Lidia's squeal and laughter no doubt carried across the terrain. Aileen meant to shush her but couldn't swallow her own mirth.

Soon the road evened, but the vehicle's wheels made an awful racket on the cobblestone street. There was no way they could pass unnoticed. Aileen peeked out the curtain again and saw a quaint village, with homes and businesses on hilly streets, as they passed. "We're in Kinsale."

"Da came here once on business and brought the family. So much to see." Lidia sniffed the air and rubbed her stomach. "Ach, and the food here is *me daza*."

Aileen's stomach grumbled, reminding her she'd eaten little at breakfast. "I'm confident we can get something to eat on the ship." Hopefully she could keep it down. She'd never been on the water, so she had no idea how it would affect her. "Have you been on the sea?"

"No. Must say I'm uneasy. I've heard steamships are loud. What if there are big waves?"

"Let's try to look at it as an adventure." Aileen tried to put a lighthearted face on, when in truth she was running away from a dreadful situation. She couldn't imagine submitting to Brian MacAuley's advances. Though this trip was for survival, it was indeed a quest. They were traveling to America and might never return.

The sky darkened, and large fat drops of rain pounded against the carriage roof. The shower became a deluge, and by the time they reached the docks, the water came down in sheets.

"Whoa!" The driver slowed the carriage, and no sooner had the coach stopped than a man yanked the door open. Aileen shrank back as a large man, covered from head to foot in a black slicker, reached in, grabbed her around the waist, and lifted her from the conveyance. In a gruff voice that matched his intimidating appearance, he muttered, "Hurry yourselves up, ladies. We're late leaving port, and our customers are beginning to ask questions."

Another man similarly dressed but not as gruff, threw a slicker over her head and pulled the hood up around her face. He also covered Lidia similarly. The ship resembled a huge gray mammoth set against the gray-blue of the harbor. They were hustled along and up the boarding ramp, where they entered through a large door in the side of the ship.

"Seal her off, mates."

"Aye aye, Captain." Two sailors by the door did his bidding.

The captain and his assistant removed their slickers and hung them on pegs along the wall. Aileen and Lidia did the same.

He spoke into a device attached to the wall. "Slow ahead, and let's get under way." Immediately the rotation of the turbines vibrated the floor. Aileen glanced at Lidia, to see her eyes bright with excitement. Butterflies danced in Aileen's stomach. She took deep breaths to calm the jitters.

The captain ushered them along a narrow passage and opened the door to a cabin. It wasn't much wider than the hall. A cot occupied each wall, separated at the head by a washstand. A locker stood at the other end, leaving a small entry space for the door. "Have a seat, ladies."

They did as asked, and he sat on the cot across from them. He drew in a deep breath. "I'm the captain of this freighter. Name's Captain Campbell."

"This isn't a passenger ship, then?" If so, they must be in third class.

"No, we're a cargo ship carrying supplies to Boston. Stopped in here to take on fresh water. Beings we're not transporting immigrants, you won't be as closely scrutinized as those on a passenger ship."

Passing immigration inspection hadn't entered Aileen's mind, not that she'd been given long to think on the subject. Though both she and Lidia were healthy, without passports they would be required to pass through checkpoints, which would be long and tiring. She'd heard horror stories of the trials their countrymen and women had faced.

"I know this room is sparse compared to what you're used to, but it is the best we could do."

"We'll be fine, Captain." Aileen nodded to Lidia. "We'll make do."

"Glad to hear it, as two of my officers gave up their bunks and moved in with the crew to give you some privacy."

"Please thank them for us."

He smiled and dipped his head. Due to the whiskers and weathered skin, his expression resembled a grimace. "Now for the rules. It won't do for my crew to know there are two women on board. Most are family men and would be respectful, but a few might try to take liberties. Those behaviors won't be tolerated; they would result in severe punishment. For the sake of peace aboard this ship, I ask that you not leave your room unless you are escorted by either my first mate, Mr. Hughes, or me."

Lidia's eyes were round as saucers. "We don't want to cause any trouble, sir." She glanced at Aileen for affirmation. Aileen nodded. She had read about harsh sentences for sailors at sea—of lashings and other atrocities.

"Indeed not, sir. We'll do as you ask," Aileen added.

"Good. I know being cooped up in here will not be easy, but at least it's winter, and you won't be hot. Let us know if you need extra blankets."

Lidia reached out and ran a hand over the bedding stacked at the foot of each bunk. "Is Mr. Hughes the man who was with you tonight?"

"Yes. If he can assist you in any way, let him know."

Aileen's stomach grumbled, and she cringed at the telling sound.

"Food will be here shortly." A tap rang on the door. "Ah, there he is now."

He opened the door to a young man in his teens. Eyes cast to the floor, the youth entered and, one-handed, unfolded a table and set it between the two bunks. His other hand held a generously laden tray of food. Delicious aromas wafted their way.

"Ladies, this is Liam, the only male allowed in your cabin. He'll see you're fed and your room is clean."

Lidia grinned. "Hello, Liam. You're the spitting image of me brother Ethan." She narrowed her eyes. "I hope you're not mischievous too. Be a shame to have to box your ears."

The boy reddened, diminishing the smattering of freckles across his nose. "Oh, no, ma'am."

"Lidia!" Aileen turned to Liam. "She's teasing you—an impish side of her I'm just now seeing. You may have to find a way to pay her back."

The tension left his shoulders, and he grinned. The captain stood and clapped the boy on the back. "Well, now, Liam will always be close if you need him. Lift the lever by the door, and a light will come on in the kitchen. We'll leave you ladies to eat and retire. You must be tired after your long journey." At the door, he turned before exiting. "Always keep your cabin locked. Since we'll be sneaking you into the city, the fewer people who know you're here, the better."

Chapter Four

Aileen stood and locked the door behind Brian and the captain. She and Lidia sat on their cots with the table between them. Surprised at the hearty fare they'd been served, they ate their fill and were full and content when they crawled into their beds.

As she lay beneath the covers thinking of all she'd left behind—Da and her friends, her home, the staff who loved her, and her homeland—tears trailed down her cheeks. She brushed them aside. *Lord, please watch over Da and keep him safe. I pray he won't repeat his mistakes.*

Her journey to freedom had begun but had little in common with the masses of emigrants leaving Ireland. Aileen's plight was entirely different. Her oppression was family oriented, forced upon her by a greedy man. As she thought more about it, her grandfather was also to blame. Why had they never met, and why hadn't he contacted her after her mother's death? In her eyes, he was a mean, bitter man, one totally without love and compassion in his heart. One day she'd tell him just that. If he'd given her a chance, she'd have loved him dearly.

One day…

****

"What do you mean she's gone? The chit told me I could come for her answer today." He sneered. "I looked forward to a sweet sample of her charms."

With his fist raised, Quinton charged, but laughing, Brian danced out of his range. "Now, now, old man. I only meant a kiss or two."

"You're disgusting, you know that?"

"Ah, I do, but in this situation, I had every right. After all, we're practically engaged."

Quinton poured a whiskey and handed it to MacAuley before filling his own glass. "She has no' given you her decision, so you have no claim on her."

"Aw, but I do. She led me to believe she'd be my mistress or my wife."

"Aileen did no such thing. You forget, you have me to throw in prison." He waved his empty hand. "So get ye gone and come back with the magistrate."

"Sorry, old chap. I've decided I want the girl, not the money." He set his glass on the mantel. "Meet me at the docks in Dublin by noon tomorrow. We'll discover which ship your daughter sailed on and her intended port. If necessary, we'll beat the information from that lawyer of yours."

Quinton waffled between being horrified and elated. Disgust washed over him as his hope of escaping time in prison once again rose.

****

Aileen and Lidia, each wrapped in their cloaks, hoods pulled securely over their heads, stepped off the gangway at Boston Harbor. The winter wind off the water whipped the wool of their capes and attacked their ankles. Although they both wore woolen hose, the icy tentacles of the freezing air penetrated the fabric. "Where are we?" The wharf was long, and, in the distance, Aileen could just make out a waiting carriage.

Though night, men worked loading and unloading cargo.

"This is India Wharf. In the morning the activity will be three times what it is now. Ah, good, the carriage is waiting. This is one place you should nay frequent—even with a big burly man like myself at your side." The captain's chuckle elicited a giggle from Lidia. "Nothing but hooligans, drunks, and, well, never mind…"

Captain Campbell handed them into the waiting carriage. "It's been a pleasure having you aboard, ladies. I regret we couldn't offer you more freedom on the ship, but…" He shrugged a massive shoulder and waved a hand.

Aileen squeezed his hand. "We appreciate your getting us here, Captain, and for taking such a risk." The cargo inspection team had come within a few feet of discovering his unlawful cargo when they docked. She didn't know what the punishment would be—a fine, or loss of admittance to enter the harbor. Thank goodness they'd remained undetected.

"Ach, I couldn't turn down Jamison's two lassies." He closed the door and gave instructions to the driver. They were in motion before they finished uttering, "Goodbye."

As they traveled through the dock area, the screech of machinery, and the shouts of men barking orders drifted through the curtained windows. Thankfully the glass kept most of the cold from invading the coach.

Away from the pier, the racket changed to boisterous laughter and slurred speech, some with heavy Irish brogues.

Aileen cringed at what sounded like curses and

jeers of encouragement, accompanied by smacks of fists against flesh. The coach blocked out the exact words—probably a good thing, too—but the tone was undeniable.

"Sounds like me two older brothers settling their differences after a pint too many." Lidia chuckled. "Suspect some of those blokes are not from home, though. Their accents are foreign."

"Your father lets the boys fight?" Aileen couldn't fathom a parent allowing such conduct.

"Sure. Tells them to take it outside before Mam takes the rolling pin to them."

****

The Jamisons welcomed Lidia and Aileen into their home and closely knit family. They insisted Aileen address them as Uncle Avery and Aunt Joan, as Lidia did. Within a week, Aileen fit in as though she'd lived there for years. Although unusual, the experience of being in a large family, surrounded by love and acceptance, helped ease her aching heart and reminded her of her mother. Their house rang with laughter. She decided to give in to her mother's wishes and no longer wore mourning. Except for periods of melancholia, Aileen was happier than she'd been since before her mother's illness and her passing.

This afternoon, two weeks after they'd disembarked, a small trunk arrived for Aileen. She sat on the bed she shared with Lidia and opened the chest Uncle Avery Jamison had carried up the stairs and set on the blue coverlet.

Inside, on top of several dresses, she found a letter from her mother. Hands shaking, she pulled the pages from the envelope and opened it to read:

My dearest daughter,

Since you are reading this, you are eighteen now, a young lady. Oh, how I'd love to be with you, to see you blossom into womanhood. I pray you're safe and happy. Due to your father's gambling, I've made arrangements with my solicitor, Mr. Jamison. Trust his counsel. He's never failed me.

I should have told you this long ago, but there never seemed to be the right time. Quinton Lynch is not your natural father. His name is Captain Joseph Chamberlain. Please don't hold hard feelings against him. We were in love and planned to marry, but he felt honor bound to return to the States and break his engagement first. For some reason his return was delayed, and when my father learned of my condition, he forced me to marry Mr. Lynch. When Joseph returned, Father sent him away with the news I'd married. He never knew about his child.

The locket I wore every day was a gift from Captain Chamberlain. Please care for it, and hand it down to your daughter. The pearls were my mother's.

Though Father never spoke to me again, Charles reported seeing him around the estate, he assumed hoping for a glimpse of you. Charles took it upon himself to load you in the pony cart and walk into the village at times he suspected Father would be there.

Mr. Lynch accepted you and loved you as his own the day you were born. He's been a good husband and father, until gambling became his pastime.

You were the joy of my life, dear Aileen. Be happy, daughter.

Your loving mother,
Maureen Callahan Lynch.

Would their lives have been different if Captain Chamberlain had returned in time? She'd been fortunate. Mr. Lynch had taught her to ride a pony, and they often rode together in the mornings. Aileen didn't doubt his love for her.

Something rattled in the envelope. Aileen peeked inside to find a small key. She lifted the wood and ormolu jewelry box from the small steamer trunk and set it on the bed before her. The key fit and unlocked the casket.

Brushing her tears away, she lifted the first velvet pouch to examine its contents. Beautiful creamy white pearls trailed from the bag, their length seeming endless. Aileen slipped the strand around her neck, and it fell almost to her waist. She didn't know much about pearls, but these were large and must have been treasured by both her grandmother and her mother.

She rifled through the various pieces—pearl earrings, a ruby brooch and ring, and a variety of pieces of lesser value. Her mother must have enjoyed wearing them, else she wouldn't have saved them. The locket rested at the very bottom. It was carefully wrapped in a lace handkerchief. Made in rose gold, the casing was slightly smaller than a guinea fowl egg.

Aileen traced her mother's intricately engraved initials on the face. On the back she found her father's. She pushed a small lever, and the locket opened to a miniature of her mother, one Aileen hadn't seen before. Another small lever opened another tiny cover, revealing a handsome man. Brown wavy hair outlined his face, with an errant curl escaped from the combed-back style and dropped to his forehead. His brown eyes gazed out at her, the seductive smile on his lips assured he had captured his audience.

No wonder you fell in love, Mam. He's a handsome man. Given her mother's auburn hair and flashing blue eyes, Aileen suspected he'd been thoroughly smitten with Mam, also. From the stories the servants told, stories common in the village, she'd had many suitors, but it was the captain who caught her heart.

Though Aileen had inherited her mother's dark auburn hair, her eyes were deep brown like her father's, and her lips curled in the same manner as did his. Lost in thought, she returned everything but the locket to the valise. She slipped its chain over her head and admired her reflection in the dresser mirror. Before her death, her mother had given her a few pieces of jewelry, but nothing to compare with the locket. The chain allowed the ornament to hug her breastbone, a comforting sensation. It would still be visible with a scooped-neck evening gown, yet was appropriate for daytime wear also.

Just as she reached to open the bedroom door, Lidia burst in. "Hurry now. Auntie Joan is holding dinner until you arrive."

They hustled down the stairs, to be met at the foot by Uncle Avery. He boomed, "Here they are, Mother." He guided them to chairs beside each other.

"I'm so sorry to hold you up. Going through my mother's things took longer than I'd expected." Unconsciously, Aileen reached up and clutched the locket.

"You are not to worry, dear. It's completely understandable." Though Mrs. Jamison smiled, her voice held a trace of sympathy.

Mealtime was a vivacious affair. The eight-year-old twin boys, Daniel and Jonathon, were anxious to finish so they could be excused, but Lidia, Aileen, and Colleen visited back and forth across the table. Colleen was anxious to show them around the city. "Father, may we take the coach tomorrow?"

"Not unless your mother is free to take you." He hit his forehead with the palm of his hand. "Ach, Joan, I forgot to tell you. Samuel Walker will be in town for a few days later next week."

Joan raised her eyebrows. "And just where will we put Sam? The house is full to bursting." She smiled. "Of course, I'm always glad to see him."

Colleen leaned across the table and hissed at Lidia and Aileen. "He's from Texas and is *so* good-looking."

Both boys burst out in laughter and made smooching noises. "Colleen's got a boyfriend, Colleen's got a boyfriend."

The girl's pale complexion flushed scarlet, and she squealed.

Uncle Avery raised his voice. "That's enough, now. Leave your sister alone." He turned to Colleen. "Regardless of how he looks, he's too old for you. You're only fifteen, and I'll not have you making eyes at him while he's here."

Colleen shot malicious glances toward Lidia and Aileen. "What about them? Same rules apply, right?"

Her father released a pent-up breath. "They are older, daughter, and I suspect they know how to behave in front of male visitors." He studied Aileen and Lidia.

Aunt Joan clapped and speared them with a glance. "I'll be working with all three of you girls tomorrow morning at ten o'clock to perfect your social skills. Be ready."

Aileen nodded to her hostess. "Yes, ma'am."

Uncle Avery wiped his mouth, placed his napkin on the table, and stood. "Good. Glad that's all worked out. And dear, I didn't mean to imply you weren't on top of the events around here. You're an excellent hostess. Don't worry about a room. Sam is staying at a hotel."

****

Fort Stockton, Texas

"Pa, Pa, please take me with you. I'll be good. I promise." Sam Walker managed to reach the buckboard, with each step dragging along his five-year-old son wrapped around his leg. He tossed his travel bag into the back and reached down to pick up his son.

Tad's arms locked around Sam's throat, choking him. The little tadpole was strong for his age. Sam pried one arm loose and held it down so he could look him in the eye. "Now, son, you know I can't. I have meetings to attend, and who'd look after you during the day?"

The boy pushed out his lower lip, dropped his head, but cast his beautiful blue eyes up. They were so much like Jane's. Sam's heart wrenched every time Tad swung them his way, especially when wanting something. "I'm big, Pa. I can take care of myself."

Sam ruffled the boy's blond hair. "I know you are, son, but the hotel won't allow it." He widened his eyes and feigned an expression of horror. "Why, they might put me in jail."

Tad's eyes rounded. "Really?"

"Well, I don't know for sure, but they could. That's what I'd do to a man if he left his little boy alone all day."

Tad released a heavy sigh and hung his head. "All

43

right. I sure don't want you to get in trouble."

Sam chucked him on the chin. "Anyway, I need time to find a surprise for you in Boston. How could I shop with you underfoot?"

Tad's mouth gaped. "A...A surprise for...me?"

Sam swallowed his chuckle. "You are going to behave for Aunt Ruth, right?"

"Yes, sir. And I'll do my chores and take a bath, too."

Sam set him on his feet. "All right, then. That settles it." He leaned down and whispered in Tad's ear. "I think Aunt Ruth needs a surprise too. Don't tell—"

Before he could finish, Tad was running and yelled, "Aunt Rufe, guess what?" Sam guffawed. So much for surprises. Ruth smiled and waved. Her pretty face held something he couldn't quite put his finger on. Was it sadness? Maybe, but he didn't think so. The woman had become a thorn in his side of late with her attempts to draw him into a romantic relationship. He stared at the young woman. All Sam wanted from a relationship at this point was friendship, and she'd begun to care for him beyond that. Though her strength had kept him going after Jane and their infant died, when he returned, he needed to distance himself from her.

"We'll be fine, Sam. Have a good trip."

Sam left the wagon at the livery and sat on a bench outside the mercantile to wait for the four o'clock stage. Within an hour he was on the coach, along with three wranglers and a traveling businessman and his wife, rocking along on the bouncing vehicle to Monahans. Thank goodness the center bench was unoccupied, so they had more leg room. Regardless, their shoulders touched, and with each hole in the road, they bumped each other. Traveling with nine souls crowded into the coach would have been torture. He didn't envy the woman across from him. Though it was winter, it wasn't that cold, and she wore a black long-sleeved traveling costume and a heavy wool coat. She must be roasting in the close confines of the cab. Plus he doubted the scented hankie held to her nose blocked out the rank odor of the dusty cowboys.

They would arrive in Monahans in time for him to board the eight a.m. Texas Pacific, and the remainder of his trip would be by rail. It would take seven or eight days. The schedules were pretty precise, so a delay would be unlikely, but you never knew.

Sam stared out the window and watched the sun set behind the Glass Mountains. Streaks of red, orange, and gold topped by a dropping curtain of turquoise eased the vivid colors behind the cliff into a black void of nothingness. Sam never tired of watching the sunsets here, or for that matter, the sunrises. To many, the desert landscape lacked beauty. To love it, you had to know and appreciate the arid country and the surprising splendor that sprang from the desert floor. There was also the heat, and the lack of social life, particularly since the fort closed in 1886. With the proposed arrival of the Southern Pacific Railroad, hopefully Fort Stockton would grow and provide some cultural activities and a hotel. Right now the only lodging was Mrs. Arbuckle's place, and she had only one room to rent.

He should never have brought Jane from her life in Boston to live here. She was a fragile flower and couldn't flourish in the heat and harsh countryside.

Between the two of them—the desert and Sam himself—they'd killed her.

Chapter Five

Sam knocked at the Jamisons' brownstone house on a residential street in South Boston. Avery answered the door. "You're here. Come in, Sam." He shook Sam's hand, turned, and called to his wife. "Joan, he's here."

The petite, dark-haired woman, brown eyes sparkling, excused herself from an older couple across the room at the buffet table and rushed over. He bent to kiss her cheek as she grasped his hands. "Sam, it's so good to see you."

"It's been too long, Joan...at least three years. When are you coming to Texas for a visit?"

"Now Sam, can you imagine traveling so far with three children, especially those rowdy boys?"

Avery extended his hand to take Sam's hat. "Can I offer you something to drink? Irish whiskey?"

Sam chuckled. "I think you can twist my arm."

Avery grinned and slapped him on the back before heading to the dining area. No doubt about it, the Irish made the best whiskey.

Joan took Sam's arm and led him toward a tall, elderly man sporting a handlebar mustache, and his tall, reed-thin wife. "Mr. and Mrs. Abernathy, this is our friend from Fort Stockton, Texas, Dr. Samuel Walker."

The older man pumped Sam's arm. "Pleased to meet you, young man."

"Likewise, sir." He turned to Mrs. Abernathy. "A pleasure, ma'am."

She flipped open an oriental fan and waved it about her face. "I'd love to see Texas, Dr. Walker, but it takes so long to get there."

"That's true, ma'am. There is the train, but it's a week's journey, give or take a day or two."

"Yes, but I've heard trains are not the cleanest way to travel. Soot comes in through the windows and attaches to everything." She tapped his arm with her fan. "Still, easier than being bounced around in a stagecoach, I'm sure."

"Unfortunately, the train hasn't reached Fort Stockton yet, so it's necessary to also ride the stagecoach in from Monahans. A stage route runs through Fort Stockton, and from prior experience, I can attest to the fact it is a most uncomfortable mode of transportation. As to the train, travel is much cleaner now, and more comfortable, since the railroad has installed ventilation windows inside the cars on the raised upper deck."

Mr. Abernathy stroked his mustache. "So, Dr. Walker, do you treat many gunshot wounds out in Fort Stockton?"

Sam swallowed his chuckle. People from the East didn't realize that Texas, though still unsettled in many areas, did have rapidly growing cities—Fort Worth, Dallas, and El Paso were a few. Fort Stockton was not, due in part to the lack of a railroad. When the fort closed in 1886, they lost a lot of trade. "No, sir, not since I left the Army in 1885. I see more abrasions from farming or ranching accidents. I do treat a few with gunshot wounds, but not many."

Avery returned with Sam's drink. "Excuse us, folks, I'd like to introduce Sam to my niece and her friend from Ireland."

"Of course. Myrtle and I need to pay our respects to Joan." They strode toward Joan as she shooed the twins from the room.

Three young women, standing by the front bay window, laughed merrily. They stopped and cast their glances toward the floor as Avery approached.

"Colleen." Sam reached for her hand. She placed it in his and dropped a brief curtsy. "My, you've grown since I was here last. In a few years, Avery, you'll have your hands full with young men calling." Her face was slimmer, and her yellow hair fell down her back in graceful waves.

"I'm almost sixteen, Dr. Walker. Don't you think that's old enough to be considered of marriageable age?" Her impish grin spelled trouble. Avery's stern scowl wiped it from her face.

Her glance left no room for doubt as to who she thought would make a good groom. "Goodness, no, Colleen. A young lady should be older when she chooses a husband."

"But I—"

"That will be enough, Colleen." Avery beamed at the young lady beside his daughter. Dark hair caught back at the sides, her deep chestnut eyes gleamed with wit. Her ready smile left no doubt she enjoyed life.

"This is my niece, Lidia Jamison. She arrived from County Cork just three weeks ago."

The young woman dipped a quick bob and held out a gloved hand. "How d'you do, sir? It's pleased to meet you I am."

"I'm honored, Miss Jamison."

Avery took the next young lady's hand and placed it in Sam's. Soft chocolate eyes emphasized the sheen of auburn hair. Her lips curved up at the corners forming a bow…very pretty. "This is Lidia's friend and our guest, Aileen Lynch." Upon contact with her soft palm, a jolt of energy shot up his arm. Shocked, he observed her face to see if she felt the sensation also.

Color rushed to her face, but she dipped gracefully and managed a shy smile. Intriguing dimples appeared on her cheeks. "A pleasure, sir."

"The pleasure is all mine, Miss Lynch." She pulled her hand from his and stepped back.

"Colleen, would you girls see if your mother needs help?" They left to do Avery's bidding.

Sam watched as they walked away. He clapped Avery on the shoulder. "I don't envy you having three lovely ladies to keep up with when young men begin to call."

"Colleen's the one I worry about. The other two are twenty and eighteen, more mature." He shrugged. "Lidia is searching for a position of some kind, maybe in a shop."

"What about the other young lady? Does she want a job, too?"

"No, we're helping her settle in here. She left Ireland to keep from having to marry a man to pay off her father's gambling debts. He wants her to marry a most despicable man."

"Can he force her to marry?"

"Not legally, but she's not twenty-one or married, so yes, he could pressure her into an unwanted marriage."

Sam shook his head. "He must be a greedy scoundrel. Let's hope he doesn't find her."

"Hopefully she'll meet some nice young man here and marry. She's well educated and comes from an upstanding family."

"Was there no one she could turn to in Ireland?"

"I don't know all the particulars, but my brother, her solicitor, implied the grandfather cut his daughter off. Never wanted to set eyes on her again." He led Sam to a corner. "Aileen would have been born out of wedlock, but her grandfather forced his daughter to marry to save his own name and face."

"She's a beautiful girl. I doubt she'll have any trouble finding a husband."

Avery rubbed his chin. "Yes, but her time isn't unlimited, and I would hate to see her marry someone she couldn't love."

"Excuse me, Uncle Avery." Aileen stood before them holding a letter. "A cable for you."

He took the letter, tore it open, and briefly read the missive. "Forgive me, Sam, I need to tend to this."

"Of course. Perhaps Miss Lynch will keep me company."

"Yes, yes. Aileen, perhaps Dr. Walker would like another whiskey."

The young woman wasn't short; the top of her head would come to his chin, the perfect height for a dance partner. Good grief, what put that idea in his head? *That Irish whiskey, Sam.*

"Can I get you another drink?"

"No, I think one is enough."

Aileen smiled and turned to leave.

"Wait a moment. Please, tell me about the lovely

locket you're wearing."

She beamed and lifted the ornament from the neckline of her dress. "This is my most prized possession. My mam left it to me." Intricate initials decorated the front. She clicked the latch to reveal a miniature portrait and held it where he could see the likeness more clearly.

His fingers stretched to lift the piece of jewelry. "May I?"

"Yes, of course."

"I say, what are you looking at, Walker?" Mr. Abernathy pushed close to Sam for a better view and peered at the portrait. "What a lovely woman. Your mother, dear?"

"Yes."

Indeed, she was a beautiful woman. "You favor her a great deal, Miss Lynch." Sam snapped it closed and rotated the locket. On the reverse side, another elaborate monogram adorned the surface and held a clasp. Her eyes displayed a slight agitation. "May I open this?"

She chewed her lower lip for a mere second before responding. "Yes. It's my father."

Sam clicked to reveal a portrait of a man in his late twenties. "You have your father's eyes, Miss Lynch, and your mother's hair. A lovely combination."

Mr. Abernathy reached for the locket. "He reminds me of someone I've met before, but I can't place him." He turned to his wife. "Myrtle, dear. Take a look at this portrait. Does he look familiar?"

"Yes, I believe he does, but I can't figure from where." Mrs. Abernathy closed the locket and let it drop to Miss Lynch's chest. "What's his name, child?"

"Joseph Chamberlain." A faint hint of pink tinged her cheeks. "I never knew him."

Myrtle stared at her husband. "Don't we know some Chamberlains here in Boston?"

"Yes, we do, but I don't remember a Joseph."

Avery joined them. "I'm sorry, but we need to call it a night. I've received an urgent wire."

"Of course. It's late," Myrtle replied.

Avery kissed Myrtle's proffered cheek.

"We had a lovely time. You must visit us soon."

"We'd be delighted."

Colleen brought their hats. Before Sam could leave also, Avery murmured in his ear, "Please stay."

After Avery closed the front door, he ordered everyone upstairs. "Joan, will you bring Sam and me a glass of whiskey into the office and join us?"

Forehead furrowed, she nodded and left to do his bidding. Sam walked with Avery to his office at the end of the short hall.

Avery's office was more like a library. Shelves of medical books lined the walls. A large leather sofa faced his desk, and a skeleton stood sentinel in the corner. Joan handed them each a glass, and they sat— Joan and Sam on the sofa and Avery behind his desk.

"What is going on, Avery? You have me worried."

Although unclear as to why he was included in this meeting, Sam wasn't worried.

"I received a telegram from Albert, my brother and Aileen's solicitor. Either Aileen's father or a thug hired by Brian MacAuley broke into Albert's office last night. They know where Aileen is, address and all, and they boarded a ship for Boston today. He'll arrive in less than a week."

"He can't have her, Avery. She's too kind and innocent to be in the clutches of that vile man." Joan sprang from her seat and paced. "What're we going to do? We could hide her with friends, or—"

"Doing so won't solve anything, Joan. We need to find her a husband. Someone we trust, who can protect her—a man who'll treat her right and not squander her money. And take her far away..." He glanced at Sam. "Like to Texas."

Sam sprang to his feet, almost spilling his drink. He tossed back the remainder and swallowed, wincing at the heat. He welcomed the burn in his chest. "What? Whoa there, Avery. I swore I'd never marry again. You know my thoughts on subjecting a woman to the harshness of west Texas. I'll not do it."

"Are you positive that's the real reason, or is it because you're not over Jane?"

"Possibly." The love between them had been special—next to impossible to find again.

"Sam, don't you think it is time to move on? Jane's been gone now...what, two years?"

"Yes, two long years to remember her screams of pain...with me helpless, able to do nothing other than sedate her." He'd never forget, and he'd *never* recover from the agony of watching her suffer, of cradling the tiny baby girl in his hands. Jane lived long enough to hold her daughter, to count her fingers and toes. An hour later, the child joined her in death.

"You couldn't control Jane's premature labor or death."

"I should have somehow stopped the bleeding, dammit."

"But you couldn't, Sam." Avery stood and walked

around the desk. His strong hand gripped and shook Sam's shoulder. "Let it go. You did everything humanly possible."

"That's easy for you to say." He waved a hand at the portrait behind Avery's desk. Joan and the children surrounded Avery, who was seated. "Look at your fine family."

Joan stood before him, her hands twisted in her skirt. "We lost babies also, Sam. Not just one, but two." Her eyes glittered with unshed tears. Avery's arm slid around her shoulder and tugged her to his side. "Love is a strange thing. It gives us great joy, but it can also break our hearts. If we hide from feeling emotion, we become dead inside and merely exist." She captured one of Sam's hands. "You deserve more, as does your son. He needs a mother—you need a helpmate. If not Aileen, then find someone else."

She reached up and patted Sam's cheek with a palm. "Why don't you join us for breakfast in the morning?" She laughed. "Be prepared. It will be a rowdy affair. The twins didn't get to visit with you tonight, so they'll try to monopolize your time tomorrow."

"Thank you for tonight's invitation, Joan."

"You're welcome anytime." She turned to her husband. "Speaking of the twins, I'm going up to check on them."

"Think about what we've said, Sam. I know it's a lot to hit you with, no notice and all, but I could tell the young lady intrigued you."

Avery walked him to the front door and added, "We don't intend to pressure you on the matter, but if there is any way you two could make a match, it would be perfect for Aileen. I'd trust you with my own daughter." He chortled and slapped his knee. "If she were older, of course."

Chapter Six

Sam ran his hand over the cool sheet covering the empty side of his bed. Yes, he was lonely, would welcome a warm body next to his, a woman to cuddle and make love to. But in doing so, his heart would be at risk. He didn't want to love again. Another loss would put his sanity in danger. He couldn't bear to lose another wife, especially to childbirth, feeling helpless to save her. He knew Jane's situation wasn't uncommon; he'd been reminded numerous times. Though many died during or shortly after delivery, the number of cases grew less every year. Would they ever have the medical knowledge to remove the risks of childbearing? Dear God, he hoped so.

Aileen's beauty and easy manner would be an asset in a wife. He'd enjoyed the short time he'd talked with her and doubted she'd be a boring companion. Tad would love her and would probably mimic her Irish lilt. He shook his head. What could she see in a man almost ten years her senior, particularly someone who'd drag her halfway across the country to a barren, hot environment? He snorted. Even if he asked her, she'd turn him down.

Sam arrived promptly at seven a.m. Both twins met him at the door. Squeals of, "Dr. Sam, Dr. Sam," echoed down the hallway.

"Da, Dr. Sam's here." They each latched onto an

arm and pulled him into the parlor.

Avery entered the room, carrying a large plate loaded with eggs and bacon. He set the platter on the table and grabbed the collar of each of the twins. "Don't pull his arms off, boys."

"We want to show him our new Parcheesi board game." Both boys' expressions pleaded with their father.

"All right, but only five minutes."

Sam swallowed his chuckle, hung his hat on the hall tree, and followed the twins upstairs to their room. They started a round, and the competition soon escalated to a noisy, competitive level. Aileen entered the room, the periwinkle blue of her dress emphasizing the sheen of her auburn hair.

Daniel popped up from the table. "Aileen! Come play with us. Dr. Sam is a whiz at this game."

"Yeah." added Jonathon. "He says we must develop a strategy. Like soldiers in a war."

She spun her gaze to Sam. Her brown eyes twinkled. "Is that so?" She placed a hand on each twin's head. "I'll play with you after lunch. Your father wants you downstairs for breakfast."

Both boys ran to the door.

"Slow down afore you fall."

Surprisingly, they obeyed. Evidently they liked and respected the young woman. Sam's admiration for her grew.

"After you, Miss Lynch." She strode out the door, and he followed her down the hall and stairs, his eyes drawn to the gentle sway of her hips. The dip of her waist left no doubt of her womanly assets.

Breakfast was a loud yet enjoyable meal. Would

his family meals resemble this if Jane and their daughter had survived? Born into an upstanding Boston family, Jane had been more reserved than many women of his acquaintance. Though she was a loving, affectionate wife and mother, she had insisted on decorum while eating meals.

When Joan stood, all three girls jumped up and helped clear the table. Avery didn't rise, so Sam kept his seat, and the family's cook freshened their coffee. Avery studied Sam over his cup, the rising steam clouding his spectacles. "Why don't you join us for church services this morning, Sam?"

"You know I'm not Catholic."

"Yes, I do, but you could escort Aileen to the Protestant church she attends, two streets over."

Against his better judgment, Sam agreed. They finished their coffee just as the ladies descended the stairs. Avery ushered his family outside and down the walk. Sam and Aileen walked in the opposite direction.

The sun shone brightly and kept the chill at bay. Aileen's hand, covered in black kid gloves to match her bonnet, felt comfortable tucked between his forearm and side. They walked briskly, surprising for a young lady. By her smiling lips and rosy cheeks, she obviously enjoyed the fresh air.

"You enjoy walking?"

"Oh, yes. I love the outdoors."

"I expect this is quite different from your village in Ireland."

"Ach, yes. Though we have some great buildings like the church ahead, they are few in number." She flashed him a smile. "But it was the hills and trails I loved to travel. Father used to say I should've been born a mountain goat. I adored the glens and cliffs that much."

As they entered the large gray brick church, the sound of people's happy chatter filled the sanctuary with a bustling resonance.

They found a pew in the middle of the church. As others squeezed in beside them, Aileen's side was against his without an inch to spare. Her face pinkened. When he slid his arm out along the pew behind her, her rosy skin flushed red. Satisfaction thrummed in his chest. She wasn't totally immune to him. To be honest, he wasn't invulnerable to her either. Her subtle scent, floral but not too sweet, floated up to his nostrils, inviting him to bury his nose in her hair.

The day's sermon left them with the message, "Trust God's wisdom in all things. He knows the desires of your heart and through the Holy Spirit will move you toward his will. He understands our fears. Turn them over to him."

****

Sitting beside this handsome man was enough to make a girl faint. His body heat cast the scent of bay rum aftershave into the air around him. When he slipped his arm across the back of the pew, Aileen had difficulty breathing. Her warm face must betray her emotions. Of course, until arriving in Boston, she'd not been exposed to anyone who could make her blush. She snorted softly at the idea of the village boys creating such an emotion in her.

Dr. Sam touched her shoulder and leaned in to whisper, "Did you say something?"

"No, no, just cleared my throat." His hand remained on her shoulder, and she welcomed the intimacy, as well as his strength. If only she could marry such a man.

As they left the church, several of the young men she'd met on previous Sundays tipped their hats and spoke. One gentleman stopped in their path. He whipped off his hat. "Miss Lynch."

"Hello, Mr. Weber. Lovely sermon today, was it not?"

"Yes, indeed."

"Let me introduce a friend of Dr. Jamison. Dr. Samuel Walker from Texas."

Dr. Sam offered his hand, and Weber grasped it. Aileen couldn't help but notice how the doctor's hands swallowed the younger man's.

"Seth Weber, Dr. Walker."

"Mister Weber."

Seth returned his attention to Aileen. "May I have the honor of calling on you?"

Flustered, Aileen felt her face warm again. Dr. Sam's expression remained stoic.

"Why, yes, Mr. Weber, that will be acceptable. Come for tea next Saturday."

He executed a slight bow. "I shall look forward to it." With a nod to Dr. Sam, Weber sauntered off down the street, twirling his cane.

****

Sam digested his thoughts about Weber as they continued their walk. So she did have eligible men interested in her, but for some reason, the idea of her marrying that dandified man didn't sit well with him. Why? Did he want to marry her himself? He swallowed a groan.

Aileen squeezed his arm. He glanced down to note

the brows above her radiant eyes were furrowed. "Do you believe God has control over our lives in the way Pastor Renfro suggested?"

"In all honesty, I'm not sure."

She nodded. "Me also, but his words make me wonder about things...like...will I escape my father's problems for now? I do hope I'll see Da one day, but I hope I never have to meet Mr. MacAuley again."

"I hope you don't either."

"Thank you. I do hope you won't think too harshly of my father. He's a good man despite his penchant for gambling."

"It's a vice that's destroyed many men and their families."

He thought about some of his reactions today—his need to touch Miss Lynch and his enjoyment of her lovely scent—and wondered if the Lord was pushing him in a direction contrary to his resolutions. He sighed. Only time would tell.

After lunch, the twins demanded Aileen hold to her promise and play Parcheesi. "Would you like to join us, Doctor?"

"Yes, I would, Aileen. May I call you by your given name?"

She smiled and nodded.

"And please, call me Sam."

The twins watched their exchange with interest. She laid a hand on each head. "Lead on, boys." They took off at a run. "Slow down afore ye break your heads."

Sam motioned to the stairs. "After you."

When they reached the landing, she stopped. "You must understand, I've had lots of practice." Her eyes twinkled with humor as she grinned, her pink lips exposing even white teeth.

To the delight of the twins, Sam puffed out his chest in mock bravado. "I think I'm up to the challenge."

Two hours and five games later, Sam was the winner of one round, loser of four. Each twin won a game, and Aileen had won two. He couldn't remember when he'd had a more enjoyable time. He'd buy Parcheesi for Tad so they could play at night.

Avery met them as they descended the stairs. "Sure was a lot of racket up there." He directed a stern stare at each twin. "Are you sure you didn't tear the roof down?"

"Oh, no, sir!"

Jonathon leaned into his father's side and chuckled. "Thing is, Dr. Sam is a sore loser."

Hand over his heart, Sam sputtered, "Am not."

"Are too," quipped Aileen, making the boys laugh.

Sam made a lunge for the boys, and they ran into the kitchen.

"Sam, can you come into my office for a minute?"

Sam sat on the leather sofa, stretched his legs out in front of him, and crossed his ankles. What now? Were his feelings not clear the previous evening?

Avery handed him a glass of whiskey and eased onto the other end of the sofa. He took a sip of his drink and then turned to Sam. "So what do you think?"

"About what?"

"About Aileen. You've spent time with her today. Surely you've noticed what a delightful young woman she is and what a good mother she'd make for Tad. I can tell you, the lass has been a steadying influence for the twins. They adore her."

Sam released the air he'd been holding in his lungs. "Avery, why do you push this notion of yours? I don't want to marry. I know you're worried about her, but you can relax. A young man from church, a Seth Weber, is calling on her Saturday."

"That namby-pamby boy? Why, he couldn't protect Aileen against a child, much less a ruthless man like this Brian MacAuley." Avery dropped his head into his hand and massaged his temples. "Aileen confided in Joan that this man gave her a choice…be his wife or be his mistress." His eyes pleaded with Sam. "Of course she'd marry the man and be tied in a loveless marriage for the remainder of her life. Plus, who knows how he'd treat her. I can't let a man like him have her. I feel in my bones he'd break her spirit and destroy her beauty in no time."

Anger shook Sam's frame. How disgusting for a man to offer a young lady such a proposition. He struggled, trying to deny his attraction to the youthful female, but the thought of her being mistreated was too much to bear. He could handle her being with the insipid Seth, but not with a man with such little respect for women.

He stood and slammed his glass on Avery's desk. "With your permission, I'll speak with Aileen now in the garden." Avery's expression of relief exacerbated Sam's guilt. "But hear this, my friend. I will not get that young woman pregnant and watch her die. It will be a marriage of convenience."

Chapter Seven

"Sam, this has to be a real marriage, one that is consummated. If Lynch found out the nuptials had not been, he might make her go through an annulment and find a way to force her to marry this MacAuley." Avery removed his glasses and massaged the bridge of his nose. He expelled a deep sigh. "You do desire her, do you not...and...uh, can execute the deed?"

A loud guffaw, laced with bitterness, rolled up from Sam's belly. "No, I'm not impotent, and yes, I do want her. What man wouldn't?" She had everything a man could want, but he was determined not to fall in love with her. Though he intended to depend on the rhythm method and use protection if necessary, things happened, and Aileen could become pregnant.

"If she agrees, we'll buy the license tomorrow and marry on Thursday. I want to start home Friday morning."

Avery stood and shook Sam's hand. "Thank you, my friend. I don't think you'll regret your decision." Hand on Sam's shoulder, he escorted him to the door. "Wait in the garden a minute, and let me speak to her first."

Sam stood gazing out on the brick sidewalk that wove through the long, narrow yard typical of those in row houses. The far end held a multitude of flowering shrubs and plants, while an area in the front was all grass, most likely as a place for the boys to run and play. It wasn't much room for active boys. Tad had acres to roam, but he gained freedom gradually…it had to be earned.

The back door opened, and he turned to see Aileen approaching. She wore her black pelisse to ward off the chill in the air. Her hesitant smile relieved his worry, and some of the tension left his shoulders. She'd been prewarned so wouldn't be taken unaware. For that he was thankful. He strode to meet her and, tucking her arm over his, led her down the path to the flower garden. A bench sat to the side, with paving stones around the perimeter to protect shoes from the dirt. "Have a seat." She smoothed her skirt, and it fell gracefully around her ankles. He sat in the space beside her and took her hand.

"Did Avery talk with you?"

"Yes, he did, and I agreed to your proposition."

Sam winced at her choice of words, but, truthfully, that is precisely what it was—a business agreement— yet he was grateful she'd accepted. "Thank you, Aileen. Though west Texas is a dry barren place—temperatures reach over a hundred degrees in the summer—the desert can be quite beautiful when the wind isn't blowing."

"I should be thanking you, Sam. You're taking me out of my father's reach and providing me with a home and a son, and hopefully more children."

"I don't—"

She lowered her eyes. "Yes, I know your position on the subject, but I hope in time you'll change your mind."

"He told you why I don't want more children?"

Her gaze met his. "Yes, but I'm strong and healthy, Sam, and I don't fear childbirth. Perhaps my attitude is naive on my part, but life doesn't hold any promises. We just have to live it." Her glance moved from their joined hands back up to his face. "I hope you'll change your mind."

He looked out across the garden, comparing it to those he'd seen at home, filled with succulents and other plants requiring little water. Either that or they had to be watered daily. Would this lovely shamrock from Ireland bloom and thrive in the arid desert? Why did this have to be so complicated? She wanted to get away from her father. He required a wife, and Tad needed a mother. What would be worse? Leaving her to deal with her father's gambling debt or his fear of her dying during childbirth?

"I admire you, Aileen, and can offer you a home, esteem, protection, and respect, but I will not fall in love. You're a beautiful woman, one who deserves to be loved. I hate to take that chance away from you. If you can live with what I'm offering, perhaps we can enjoy a successful marriage."

****

The train station platform bustled with people bidding loved ones goodbye. The whistle sounded, and the conductor's shout, "All aboard!" sent people scurrying to the vestibules to board the train. Aileen bit back tears as she waved at Lidia and the Jamisons one more time. In the two short months she'd been in Boston, they'd become her family. Though happy when her mother lived, she'd not had the joy of brothers and sisters. She'd miss them. Sam must have heard her sniffles, as his hand palmed her shoulder and squeezed her to his side. His breath against her ear as he whispered reminded her of their intimacy last evening.

"You'll see them again and can send letters back and forth."

She dabbed at her tears with her handkerchief. "I know. It's just they're the only true family I've experienced since my mother died."

His deep voice rumbled. "Now you have me and Tad."

Yes, the idea brought a smile and lightened her mood. And with any luck, after their coming together last night, their family would grow. She blushed at the memory of Sam's lovemaking. Joan had tried to prepare her for what to expect, but Aileen guessed it was something one needed to experience to fully understand. There was a small amount of pain, but the pleasure well made up for the discomfort. Would they do that again tonight? She hoped so.

She peeked at him from under her bonnet. "And, with any luck we'll have more children—playmates for Tad."

He removed his arm from around her. Face closed, he said, "We'll see," and turned his gaze to their fellow travelers.

A couple came through the car, the man and his wife carrying parcels that bumped people along the way. "Excuse me...Pardon...Sorry." One bump knocked Sam's hat askew. He jerked it from his head as Aileen stifled a giggle.

"I'm grateful I was able to book us into first class. I can't imagine what second class must be like right now."

Aileen enjoyed all the activity, though not being

jostled. Never had she seen so many people and such a variety all at one time. And the accents...she'd heard at least four. She recognized Scottish as well as English, and of course, Irish. The others she couldn't identify. She grasped Sam's arm. "I find this all very interesting."

"It will grow old by the end of our journey."

She couldn't imagine getting tired of the activity, but didn't say so. "How long do you think the journey will take?"

"If there is no trouble making connections, we should make it to Abilene in five days—give or take a day. We'll spend a few nights there so you can shop and rest up for the last leg of the trip."

Apprehension twisted in her belly. Would Tad like her? And Sam's housekeeper... Aileen's skills were limited. She feared she'd not be of much use. In time, she hoped to take over some of the chores. Sam had assured her that Rosa would teach her.

She glanced down at the plain gold ring on her finger. With her thumb she moved it around and around. It would take a while to grow used to, but the fit was good. She wouldn't need to worry about losing the band. Along with her locket and pearls, the ring was now one of her most prized possessions.

Sam captured her hand. "Does your ring fit well enough?"

"Yes, it's perfect."

"I'm sorry there wasn't time for you to pick it out."

"It's just what I would have chosen, but I would like for us to get the date engraved inside."

"That'll be easy enough to take care of in Fort Stockton."

****

Sam escorted Aileen to the dining car for lunch. To walk there, they had to pass through a drawing room. Several travelers sat in the comfortable chairs reading. A few women worked on needlework. He couldn't help but smile at Aileen's joy in everything. "Oh, I wish I'd brought a project—embroidery or tatting."

"Perhaps we'll have a layover and you can shop, buy handkerchiefs and other supplies."

The porter beckoned them forward and held Aileen's chair. She slid into her seat, laid her napkin over her lap, and leaned forward. "This is so exciting. I was pretty much confined to the house after my mother's illness turned bad. Before that, when she was well, we often went to Cork for the day."

"Can I ask what form of illness your mother had?"

Her bottom lip trembled. "It was a cancer." She drew in a deep breath. "It was inoperable."

He reached across and clasped the hand fisted on the table. "Ah, I see. I'm so sorry."

She tried to smile, but the expression didn't quite meet her eyes. "'Tis all right. Her passing was a release for her…an end to her pain. I must be grateful to God for her relief."

"I'd liked to have met her. From your lawyer's account, she was a fine lady and a good business woman."

A smile lit up her face. "Aye, that she was."

When Sam had received the telegram with the details of Aileen's inheritance, the amount was staggering. No wonder Aileen's mother didn't want her husband frittering it away. Fortunately Fort Stockton had a bank, and Sam's lawyer would manage the money. He didn't intend to touch the capital. It was hers, though who knew what she'd be able to spend it all on.

Their food arrived, and they were quiet for a while, listening to the voices of those around them. Sam ordered coffee with his meal. Aileen drank hot tea. "Do you like coffee?"

She smiled over the rim of her cup. "I like it somewhat, but not as well as tea. Mayhap in time I'll learn to be a coffee drinker."

He chuckled. "Don't force yourself on my account."

They returned to their seat. Sam studied some of the medical journals he'd bought at the conference. He was anxious to read one in particular on diagnosing diabetes. Aileen watched the passing countryside as the train flew down the tracks. The wife of the couple sitting across from them engaged her in conversation about fashion. Sam tuned them out, as he assumed the lady's husband did also.

Sometime later, Aileen interrupted his train of thought. "What is your home like, Sam?"

He closed his pamphlet. "The house is built in the same style as the officer's quarters at Fort Stockton, but ours is U-shaped. It's not large but is a comfortable one-story home built of adobe bricks made of clay, straw, and sand. The bricks help cool the house in the summer and hold heat in the winter, so they are perfect for building in the hot, dry climate. After the blocks dry and the house is built, stucco is applied to give the exterior a smooth finish. Then it is painted. The floors are clay tile and wood." It was different from any of the homes in Boston and, he assumed, in Ireland also.

"Don't forget, my dear, it is your home too. You're welcome to change anything you like...except my office."

"It sounds lovely. I'm sure I won't wish to change much."

"I hope you feel the same way after you see the place, as it's nothing fancy."

****

Aileen stepped from the washroom wearing her robe with only her chemise underneath. She wanted to be able to dress quickly if need be. Her traveling costume was folded and stored in her portmanteau. It would slide under their bed in case she needed it in a hurry. Sam waited for her right outside the door and walked her to their berth. The porter already had the seats folded down and the bed made. The couple that had sat across from them was settled in the bunk above.

Sam held the curtain for her while she crawled across the mattress. He removed his clothes and laid them across the foot of their bed. He slipped under the covers in his drawers. Suddenly shy, Aileen clutched the robe closer to her body.

He untied her robe. "You can't sleep in that. You'll get too hot and become tangled when you try to turn over." She had to admit the car was rather warm. Sam mentioned something about a hot-air furnace. "Come on, give it here." He took the robe and tossed it to the end of the bunk. When she'd settled under the covers, he slipped an arm under her head and pulled her close. Her heart thundered in her chest. Surely he'd not make love to her here. She'd die of embarrassment. "Good night, Aileen."

"Night." She released a sigh of relief but felt a

72

nagging disappointment. The thought of such an activity in these close confines brought forth a giggle.

"What's funny?"

"Sleeping this close to other people is so odd. Lydia is the only person I've ever shared a bed or even a room with." *And now I'm sharing a bedroom with close to two dozen people.* Sam's heart thrummed away under her ear, and the faint aroma of his aftershave tickled her nostrils. She fidgeted, trying to decide what to do with her free arm. The obvious remedy would be to throw it across Sam's chest, but she didn't want him to think her brazen. Finally, he made the decision for her. He took her arm, placed it across his middle, and stroked it with a gentle motion. She closed her eyes, enjoying the closeness and his touch.

"You settled...comfortable?"

"Yes, thank you. Good night, Sam."

He squeezed her with his strong arms in response. She listened to the sounds around her—snoring, coughing, and the occasional passing of gas. Not having slept in such close confines before, the intimate sounds were foreign to her. Though Sam didn't love her, lying wrapped in his embrace she experienced security for the first time since her mother's passing. A tear leaked from her eye, and she wiped it away. *No looking back, Aileen. Mother wanted you to be happy.* Aileen would make that happen.

Chapter Eight

Sam punched the pillow with his fist and observed a loose feather shoot up, hang in midair, and then drift back toward the bed. It landed atop Aileen's head, the white down a stark contrast to the dark auburn locks. Last night she'd plaited the long strands into a fat braid that hung almost to her waist. This morning, loosened wisps curled around her face. She lay on her side, her head on his shoulder. His arm tingled from lack of circulation, but he'd let her sleep a moment longer. He enjoyed watching the rise and fall of her chest...and hearing the soft flutters passing from her pretty bowed mouth.

He lifted the feather from her hair and brushed it against her nose. She batted at the small plume. He stifled a chuckle and tickled her lower lip. Her hand came up and caught him under the nose. "Oww!"

Her eyes popped open to see him holding her fist. "Trying to break my nose, woman?"

"Did I hit you?" Her grin was decidedly mischievous.

"You most certainly did."

"Sorry." She stretched, tugging her hand from his as she raised both arms above her head. They hit the padded seat back behind them. "You shouldn't tease a girl when she's asleep."

He waved the feather in front of her face. "How

about when she's awake?" Before she could react, he pulled her close and planted his mouth on hers. She started for a second and then softened against him. His lips teased and sampled hers, inviting them to open for a deeper exploration. Her arm circled his back and pulled him closer. Loving this woman would be so easy. Invisible ice water struck the back of his neck and inched down his spine. That was not going to happen; he refused to open himself up for further pain. He broke the kiss and pulled back. Voice harsh, he clipped, "It's time to get up." He didn't mean for the words to be so curt, but fear was a strong motivator.

Aileen's smile wilted. Guilt struck Sam. He wanted to soften his tone, but he didn't want to give her false hope. He sat up, reached to the foot of the bed for Aileen's dressing gown, and handed it to her.

Refusing to meet his gaze, she accepted it, but folded her robe neatly. "If you'll hand me my portmanteau, I'll get dressed here and then visit the washroom."

"All right." He lifted the bag from under the bed and placed it atop the sheet. "I'll wait for you to dress and then walk there with you." This had been their routine for the past three mornings.

"There is no need. I'll be perfectly fine on my own."

He'd hurt her feelings...or made her mad. Couldn't be helped. With his back to her, he yanked on his shirt, pulled on his pants, and stepped into his boots.

"Suit yourself." Self-reproach twisted his stomach. His actions were no way to treat a lady, especially his wife. He stuffed his shirt in and fastened his pants. "I'm waiting, Aileen. Take your time."

Five minutes later, she passed through the curtain, carrying her valise in one hand, her handbag in the other. Eyes red rimmed, she ignored him. He caught her to him in a hug. "Aileen, I'm sorry. It's not you. It's me." *And my fear.*

She didn't speak but nodded, turned, and walked toward the lavatory. He continued on to the men's restroom in the next car. As clean as possible without a tub, freshly shaven, and wearing clean clothes, he waited in the aisle for her, squeezing against the wall as people walked back and forth.

****

Aileen struggled to be congenial during breakfast, but hurt clogged her throat. Sam's expression echoed her mood. She must get beyond her wounded feelings. He'd been upfront from the beginning—he wasn't going to fall in love with her. Their time on the train had been enjoyable. They seemed to get along so well and enjoyed each other's company. She'd given in to false hope.

Either be miserable at every little slight, Aileen, or get over it and enjoy what you have—a husband, a son, the opportunity for a new life in Texas, and freedom from Father's situation.

As she sipped her tea and nibbled at her buttered toast, she surveyed the wooded landscape rushing by. Evergreen trees added color to the orange and brown leaves of deciduous trees. The leaves covered the ground, making a soft carpet. A small rivulet of water twisted through the foliage, appearing for a short while before disappearing again.

The strain between them tugged on her nerves, but her mind was made up: she wouldn't let this morning's

76

moment of intimacy happen again. Her heart couldn't take the rejection. Now, she must relay her feelings to Sam on the matter. She finished her breakfast and placed her napkin beside her plate. His plate wiped clean of the breakfast of egg, ham, potatoes, and biscuits, Sam poured another cup of coffee from the carafe on the table.

He glanced up to see her watching. "Would you like more tea?"

"Yes, thank you."

He touched the pot to check its warmth before filling her porcelain teacup, and then picked up his coffee by the bowl. No doubt his large hands made lifting by the dainty handle difficult. They drank in silence.

"Look, Aileen." He set his cup down, and the saucer rattled at the disturbance. "I'm sorry if I hurt you, but I'm trying to protect us both here."

"Really?" Heat rose from her neck up her face. Why, the audacity of the man. "Don't worry about me, Dr. Walker. From now on, I'll be taking care of myself."

Furrows formed in his forehead. "And what is that supposed to mean, Mrs. Walker?"

"It means you'll not get close enough to me for misunderstandings."

He leaned over the table and hissed, "Are you saying you'd deny me my marital rights?"

Elbows on the table, she inched forward to meet his glare. "Of course not, but I sure don't intend to actively participate or enjoy the experience."

His jaw dropped, and Aileen believed the expression in his eyes radiated regret. Her throat constricted. She had to leave. "Please excuse me." She struggled to scoot back, the chair leg catching on the carpet. He rushed around the table to assist her. Without another word, she hurried to the ladies' dressing room.

****

Sam sank back into his chair and watched as Aileen left the dining car. He dropped his head to his hand and massaged the temples. That had not gone well.

At a tap on his shoulder, he jerked around. The man at the table behind him graced Sam with a knowing grin of sympathy. "Have a little tiff with the wife?"

"No, we're fine."

He harrumphed. "Well, just in case, a little posy or gewgaw always works to smooth things over."

From the sour expression on the portly man's face, he probably purchased trinkets on a regular basis. "Thank you. I'll take your suggestion under consideration."

The gentleman patted Sam on the shoulder. "Glad to help, young man, glad to help."

Sam sure didn't intend to make a habit of buying Aileen baubles every time she got out of sorts with him. He didn't believe in squandering money on bribes. Anyway, he'd not pander to a woman's moods and whims. *That's not fair, Sam. She's been a fine traveling companion, not moody or emotional.* He'd give her a little time, and maybe she'd thaw.

Feeling somewhat better, he left the dining car. Aileen sat, sewing in her lap, in one of the wingback chairs in the ladies' parlor. She'd been able to purchase a few stitching supplies at their last stop. Her emerald green traveling suit and matching hat set off her auburn hair and dark eyes. No doubt about it, his wife was a striking woman. He'd seen admiration in the eyes of the other men travelers, and disgruntled glares from some of the jealous women. He stood at the door for a moment and surveyed her before striding to where she sat.

She blended beautifully with the Victorian decor. The climbing vines and roses covering the walls were a bit overpowering to Sam. He'd grown accustomed to the calming earth tones of the adobe and stucco walls of West Texas. With her coloring, Aileen would, without a doubt, complement the muted watercolors of the Texas landscape.

He stopped beside her. She glanced up and forced a smile. "I'll be in the smoking car if you need me." She arched an eyebrow. Unable to resist her challenge, he leaned down and kissed her forehead before striding to the car exit.

At the exit, he overheard one of the ladies trill, "My dear, your husband is a fine-looking man." He couldn't resist drawing himself up taller and puffing out his chest, but instantly wilted at Aileen's snort. The utterance was so out of character for her he had to swallow a guffaw, which resulted in a coughing spasm.

The next two days followed the same routine. Aileen was congenial during the day, particularly during meals, but at night she turned her back to him and scooted close to the wall. He'd often wake to find her curled against his back, and when he enfolded her in his arms, she snuggled closer. The minute she awoke, she collected herself and moved away.

Aileen spent her mornings with the ladies. Sam

spent his with the men. Today he'd removed himself from the gentlemen's car, as his eyes burned from the accumulation of cigar smoke. The upper vents helped considerably to clear the air, but if someone complained about the cold draft, they were closed. They were nearing Texas, and temperatures would increase somewhat if they didn't encounter snow in Oklahoma and north Texas.

It was almost time for lunch, so he stopped by to escort Aileen into the dining car. The porter seated them at a table closer to the front of the car, which gave them a better view of the other diners. They were a hodgepodge of people—some well-to-do businessmen and their wives, ranchers, some cowboys, and farmers. Most were friendly. A few rather arrogant individuals were quick to let others know their status. He'd recognized attitudes of resentment and disdain toward Aileen. Her brogue, though cultured, clearly labeled her Irish. Some couldn't get past their prejudice, which was one reason he rarely left Aileen alone. He didn't want her exposed to rudeness or disparaging remarks. And there was also an odd assortment of men who tried to apply their charms to the unattached women. Oh, he'd seen the interest in the eyes of a few. A stare from him, and they turned their attention elsewhere.

As they stepped into the dining car, the tantalizing aroma of roast beef reached his nostrils, and his stomach growled in appreciation. They'd just been served when their porter stopped and leaned toward him.

"Dr. Walker, beggin' your pardon, sir, for interruptin' your lunch."

From the furrows in George's forehead, his worry

was evident. "A gentleman in third class is very sick. High fever and such…moanin' and groanin'."

"I'm happy to take a look at him." Sam placed his napkin by his plate. "Aileen, will you have our waiter keep my plate warm until I can return?"

"Of course." Her gentle smile reassured him.

He glanced around the car to see who all was there. "Stay here until I return, all right?"

"I will. I'll be just fine."

He followed George through the cars. The porter unlocked the baggage compartment in their section, and Sam retrieved his medical bag. His patient, a thin, balding man, lay on a cot in a space made for him in the third-class storage area. A woman he assumed was the man's wife sat on a stool at his head and replaced the damp rag on his forehead with a fresh one.

"This be Mr. and Mrs. Jonas, Doctor. Folks, this is Dr. Walker."

Mrs. Jonas twisted her hands and dropped them to her lap. Her eyes glazed with misery, she murmured, "We don't have no money to pay you."

He patted her hand. "Let's not worry about that right now." Sam listened to the man's heart. The rate was high, as was his respiration rate. "How long has he been feeling bad, ma'am?"

"'Bout three days ago he couldn't hold much food down, but he didn't have the pain in his belly or fever until this morning."

Sam removed the thermometer from his bag. Mr. Jonas' temperature was 102. "Help me loosen his trousers, so I can take a look at his abdomen."

Mr. Jonas' eyes filled with panic. He raised his arms over his belly to prevent Sam from coming closer.

"Don't touch me, Doc. It…it hurts something terrible."

"I'll be careful, but I think you may have appendicitis. I need to examine you to know." It would have been helpful to have a microscope handy to examine the man's blood. Then his diagnosis would be more accurate. Nonetheless, he'd do his best without one. With his fingers, he lightly applied small amounts of pressure to the man's lower abdomen. Mr. Jonas tried to bear the discomfort, but when he yelled out in pain, Sam stopped.

"It's my opinion, Mr. Jonas that you have appendicitis. If I'm correct, you need surgery. If the appendix ruptures, the outcome could very well be fatal." Sam turned to the porter.

"George, what is our next stop?"

"Denton, Texas, sir. Arrive 'bout eight tonight."

"Mr. Jonas, you must get off the train in Denton and go immediately to a hospital." He withdrew a small envelope and handed it to the woman. "Give him two of these every four hours with a full glass of water. They'll help with the fever and pain." Sam closed his bag. The click startled Mrs. Jonas, and she jumped. "And ma'am, get someone to help you get him out of these clothes and into a nightshirt. He'll be much more comfortable."

She clutched the pills to her chest and bobbed her head. "I'll do so right away. Thank you. We're much obliged for your help."

"Glad to be of service, ma'am."

George took his bag. "I'll lock this back up for you, sir."

As they exited the storage area into the third-class car, passengers shouted questions.

"Is it smallpox…the flu?"

"Are we all gonna get sick, Doctor?"

Sam held his hand up for quiet. "Mr. Jonas is not contagious. He has appendicitis and needs surgery as soon as possible." He glanced up and down the rows. Passengers on both sides wore expressions of concern, others disinterest. "Some of you might help Mrs. Jonas in caring for her husband, so she can get some rest. And, gentlemen, he'll need to be carried off the train in the morning." Heads nodded in agreement, and a couple of women rose and stepped toward the storage room, the rhythm of the train turning their walk into a stagger.

He stopped by the lavatory and washed his hands before continuing on to the dining car. As a raised voice railed in anger, "Get your dirty Irish self back to third class where you belong. That's all your breed is good for—cleaning up after your betters," Sam froze in place.

Chapter Nine

Aileen shrank back in her chair, as far back from the rude portly man as she could move. Not only did his spittle travel her way, but also his breath, which stank. From his clothes, and the fact that he was in the first-class dining car, he must not be poor or indigent. What was it with some men? Sam's breath didn't smell bad.

Drawing herself up to her full seated height, she snatched a fork off the table and prepared to defend herself. She'd seen the signs on businesses in Boston—"NO IRISH NEED APPLY"—but couldn't imagine the prejudice following her to the West.

He grasped her arm and tugged. "Get back where you belong…with the other immigrant trash."

A screech escaped her mouth, and she aimed for his arm. A bellow halted her action.

"Take your hands off my wife." Before the man could respond, he was grabbed by his lapels and shoved. He couldn't slow his backward momentum, and, arms flying, peddled down the length of the car and landed on his bum, feet splayed in the aisle.

"Sam?" He stood beside her, his fists raised, face red, and his gaze fixed on the stout man.

"Get up, you piece of scum."

The man scrambled to his feet and charged. Before he reached him, Sam's fist caught the boorish man on the jaw and sent him flying again.

"Don't ever touch my wife again! Don't look at her and don't speak to her! Do you understand?"

As he wiped blood from his lip, the man nodded. Sam glanced around at the other diners, several of whom were men. "How could you sit here and let this man abuse my wife?"

Cautious glances were exchanged before a gentleman broke the silence. "Mister, it happened so fast, all we could do was gape." He looked at his wife and then to Aileen. "Ma'am, we apologize for not being able to prevent Mr. Boyd's bad comportment."

"Thank you, sir, but you're not to blame. The man was beside me...like he'd popped up out of nowhere. I didn't have much time to react myself."

A woman—she assumed Mrs. Boyd, by the frown of disapproval on her face—and a porter helped the stout man up. He blustered and shook them off. His wife wasn't having any of it. She gripped his arm and pinched the underside.

He straightened and yelped. "That hurt, woman."

"Got your attention, didn't it? Now, you will apologize to the young woman, and we'll take our leave."

Mr. Boyd studied Aileen and then turned to catch Sam's expression of scorn. He turned back to her and cleared his throat. "Ma'am, I beg your pardon for my improper actions." Sam didn't bat an eye, but she guessed he was satisfied. He stepped aside so the older couple could pass, talking as they went.

"I've never been so embarrassed in my life. I'd like to crawl under a rock and hide. Why, by dinner, everyone on this train will know about your outburst. We'll be a laughingstock."

"Oh, hush up, woman. You're giving me a headache."

Their voices trailed off as they left the dining car. Diners went back to their meals. Sam slid into the chair facing Aileen. He took her hand and squeezed. "I'm sorry, my dear. I never dreamed something like that would happen in here."

"You're not to blame, Sam. There was much bitterness toward the Irish in Boston. I guess it's to be expected to follow us out West."

Their waiter brought Sam's dinner, a wet towel to clean his hands, and first aid supplies. "Thought these might come in handy, sir."

"Much obliged."

Aileen pulled his hand across the table. "Here, let me wash the blood off your hand."

He squeezed her hand. "Make it fast, if you can. I'm starving."

"Should we put a bandage around your knuckles?"

After a cursory inspection, he shook his head. "No, let's leave it open to the air." He raised her hand and kissed her fingertips. "Thank you, sweetheart."

At the endearment, her heart flipped in her chest. *Calm yourself, Aileen. It's just a word.* "You're welcome." She observed him as he ate. He appeared to enjoy the roasted meat and vegetables. "Sam, you didn't need to fight Mr. Boyd like you did."

He dropped his fork to his plate and wiped his mouth with the white linen napkin. His expression changed from satisfaction to annoyance. "No man will verbally or physically abuse you while I'm around. If I hadn't seen him in the act, and later learned of the offense, I'd have hunted him down." Even though she didn't approve of fisticuffs, she'd been flattered and honored by his action. His mien softened, and he winked. "What would you have done if he'd yanked you from your chair and dragged you off somewhere?"

She held up her fork. "I was ready to puncture his abundant belly and release some hot air."

****

Aileen watched from their seat as Sam stood outside on the platform and talked with his patient before several porters slid their sick passenger into a waiting ambulance. A wire from the conductor had informed the hospital to have transportation waiting for the train. A woman stood next to Sam, her shoulders shaking as she sobbed into a handkerchief. Sam patted her shoulder and bent closer to speak with her. At the same time he pulled some bills from his pocket and folded the woman's hand over the money. She nodded and wiped tears from her face as she was helped into the ambulance.

Aileen smiled, and her heart warmed at her husband's generosity and kindness. He might not be in love with her, but he cared about her and liked her. Of that she had no doubt. Could she live with a marriage based on respect and consideration, without his deep affection? Did she have a choice? Not really, as she cared for him too much, plus she had nowhere else to go. And she'd known his feelings from the beginning and still agreed to the arrangement. So, if ever unhappy, she only had herself to blame. There was always her money, but she didn't want to view life that way…money could not buy love.

Sam returned and slid into the seat beside her. He wrapped his arm around her shoulders and squeezed.

"Are you all right?"

"Of course. Why wouldn't I be?"

"I just want to make sure you're not dwelling on Mr. Boyd's uncouth conduct earlier today." His hand moved up and down her arm in a soothing motion. Aileen had to admit she enjoyed his attention and concern. She laid her cheek against the curve of his shoulder and snuggled into his warmth. The aroma of his subdued toilet water, mingled with his natural scent, made a heady brew.

"You're sweet to be concerned, but Mr. Boyd's behavior and attitude are like many Americans who resent the Irish. In Ireland, many resent those of prosperous families. Such men are bullies to the core."

Aileen couldn't comprehend what her life would be like if she'd stayed in Ireland and married Mr. MacAuley. She shuddered, and Sam nestled her a little closer to his side. With the assistance of her mother and Mr. Jamison, God had found a safe haven for her. Now she had Sam. *Please, God, let him learn to love me. And his son—I pray he'll like me.*

"It shouldn't be long now before we pass through Fort Worth. You'll be surprised how big the cattle town is now. We'll stop, and many passengers will depart, while others will board to travel farther west. I'd considered a couple of days' stay in Fort Worth, a honeymoon of sorts, but I'm anxious to get back to Tad." He tucked a loose strand of hair behind her ear. "I hope you're not too disappointed."

Her heart plummeted. "I'd be lying if I said I wasn't…but I understand your need to see your son." If Tad were her child, she'd feel the same. She gazed out the window. As they neared Fort Worth, the size of the town became apparent by the multitude of lights flickering in the distance. It would have been fun to explore the town and maybe spot a real cowboy in action at the stockyards. Who was she kidding? Fort Stockton probably had its share of cowboys working cattle. "What about clothes? I need to buy appropriate clothing for the warmer climate."

"I've not forgotten. We'll lay over in Abilene and stay at the T&P Hotel & Eating Train Depot. Abilene is big enough to have several dry goods stores. You don't need anything fancy." He winked. "Your wardrobe is filled with fancy dresses suitable for church and the occasional party. You need sturdy shoes, boots, cotton undergarments and dresses, and riding skirts."

Riding skirts...must be women didn't wear habits here in the West.

****

Aileen could only stare at the landscape. Oh, there were trees, a few tall oaks and a lot of scraggly trees that grew warped and had strange leaves. Some kind of cactus grew among the other plants in the dirt and sand. In certain areas, the grass was sparse, in others prairie grass spread over the land and danced with the breeze. Big round bundles of dried foliage rolled across the plain when the wind blew. The countryside wasn't ugly, by any means, but it was different from anything she'd ever seen.

Sam had a mischievous glint in his eye. "Take a good look at the few oak trees and sparse greenery, as this will change again as we leave Abilene. There will be some, but the terrain will flatten out. The few hills we'll pass will be mesas or buttes. They're flat on the top, like a table."

Aileen couldn't visualize what he was describing, but she looked forward to seeing these tabletop mountains of which Sam spoke. He named trees and other foliage as they passed—mesquite trees, prickly pear cactus, and tumbleweeds. "Is there any place out here that resembles the greenery of Ireland?"

"As a matter of fact, yes. The trail from Fort Davis to San Solomon Springs, when we've had a wet year, looks somewhat like your homeland—it's an area of green in an arid environment."

"How far is it from Fort Stockton?"

"Too far for a day trip. It's a beautiful place, though, and has a great swimming hole. It's spring fed, so the water is cold. Tad would love to camp there some weekend."

Aileen had never camped out. It might be fun.

Sam leaned over and pointed out the window. "Look just ahead, and you'll see Abilene as it comes into view."

They sped by fields with cattle grazing peacefully. In the distance, blue skies reigned over craggy red rock formations and grasslands. Buildings loomed ahead, and Aileen craned her neck trying to spot the depot. The train slowed and turned onto a feeder track...right in the middle of town.

"Abilene, folks. We have a two-day layover." The conductor walked down the car giving instructions. "Hotel and good food is up the track a short ways, at the Texas & Pacific Hotel & Eating Train Depot. If you need any assistance, ask one of the porters."

Sam stood and assisted Aileen to her feet. Walking on steady ground would be awkward for a short while, an experience she'd missed. He lifted their bags, along with the medical bag George handed him on their way out.

George helped Aileen down the steps to the wooden platform. "I'll bring the Missus' small trunk up to the hotel shortly, Doctor."

Sam handed him some bills. "Thank you, George. Just leave it downstairs at the desk, and I'll carry it up later. I hope we'll see you on the next leg of our trip."

With a big smile, George tipped his hat. "Sure will, sir. Have a nice rest now."

Sam transferred all three bags to his left arm and with his right palm at her waist, directed her down the dirt road. She swayed, and chuckling, he held her waist tighter. "Can you manage the short distance up the road?"

"Of course. I just feel a bit wobbly." She stopped and reached for one of the bags. "I can carry something."

"No need, sweetheart. You may need your hands to hold your hat down."

She looked up to see a wall of sand blowing her way. Gripping her hat, she looked down to keep the dust from blinding her. After it passed, a stray twirling whirlwind danced their way. Sam hugged her face to his chest as it swirled around them, sand and dust getting into her eyes and nose. She sneezed.

"Your first dust devil, sweetheart. Welcome to West Texas."

****

Boston

Joseph Chamberlain tapped on the roof of the carriage, and the driver stopped. He studied the brownstone building in South Boston. This must be the place. He was on the right street, and there were the house numbers. Joseph had been in a state of stress ever since a Mr. Abernathy, a friend of his father's, had rushed into their shipbuilding office and asked to speak to him. He was busy, but at the man's insistence, he made time and invited him into his office.

He waved toward the leather sofa and chairs on the back wall, while his gaze wandered back to his desk covered with plans for a new ship…drawings he wanted to return to. "Have a seat, Mr. Abernathy."

His clerk rose from the desk by the door. "Shall I bring coffee, Mr. Chamberlain?"

"Yes, that would be nice, Luke." He cocked a brow at his guest. "How about you, sir?"

"It would hit the spot right now. Thank you." He sat on the sofa, and Joseph took one of the chairs facing him.

Their coffees arrived, and Mr. Abernathy asked how business in the shipping industry was faring. They discussed the economy for a few minutes while they drank their coffee. Joseph set his empty mug on a side table, and Luke came over to take it. "Now, what can I do for you, sir?"

Mr. Abernathy handed his cup to Luke, rested against the sofa cushions, and entwined his fingers over his spare abdomen. "I attended a party at Dr. Avery Jamison's home several weeks ago. He had a lovely young woman, just over from Ireland, staying with his family."

Joseph couldn't envision where this disclosure was going. "She was a charming lass, with auburn hair and lively brown eyes, almost hazel."

"Sir, I'm really busy and don't understand how this

can relate to me." He made a move to stand.

His guest held up a hand. "Hear me out. Won't take long." Joseph leaned back in his chair and waited. "She wore a gold locket that caught the attention of everyone in the room. It held delicate etching around the border and in the middle the initials M C in intricate script. The back had the same detail, but the letters were J C."

Joseph clutched at his chest in an effort to slow the pounding of his heart. "Lu...ke. Water."

He drank half of the glass and returned his attention to Mr. Abernathy.

"You're mighty pale. You feel well enough to hear the rest of this, Mr. Chamberlain?"

"Yes, yes. Go ahead."

"Inside the ornament were miniature portraits of her mother and father. Her mother is deceased, and the young woman never knew her father, but said his name was Joseph Chamberlain."

****

Joseph rapped on the door of the brownstone. He'd sent a note around yesterday to ask when he might call. His pocket watch read just at three o'clock. After all these years, he would see a child of Maureen's, perhaps his own child. The possibility had him elated yet nervous. What if it was all a mistake, and the young woman had bought the locket at a pawnshop? No, even though he and Maureen had been separated, she'd never have parted with the adornment unless—Dear Lord! He prayed she'd not sold it to buy food for their child.

The door opened, and Joseph jerked back to the present. "Mr. Chamberlain, come in, come in. My wife and I are delighted Mr. Abernathy was able to contact you." He closed the door and offered his hand, giving Joseph a hearty shake. "I'm Avery Jamison, and this is my wife, Joan."

"Pleased to meet you, Jamison, Mrs. Jamison." He bowed to the petite, dark-haired woman. She took his hat and hung it on the hall tree in the foyer.

"Come in and have a seat. I've made tea and coffee."

"If you want something stronger, I can get—"

"No, no, coffee is fine for me." Of course, after hearing what the Jamisons had to say, he might wish he'd had a shot of whiskey.

When Joseph left an hour later, he'd made up his mind to travel to Texas and hopefully arrive before Mr. Lynch and this Mr. MacAuley. He couldn't wait to get his hands on the odious man. It hurt to hear Maureen had been forced into marriage, and he was furious that her father had denied him the knowledge of their coming child. Thank goodness the man she married had loved her and their child, though his judgment concerning the daughter's future was lacking. His determination to marry her off to this MacAuley fellow wouldn't do.

I will find my daughter.

****

Aileen stretched in the large feather bed—a big difference from the pallet kind of cot they'd shared on the train. She turned over and closed her eyes…just a minute longer. At the splash of water, she opened her eyes a slit to see Sam, shirtless, at the washstand, shaving. She could see his muscles move with each motion of his arms. Fascinating. Last night, at Sam's encouragement, she had run her hands over the hills and valleys of his torso. He seemed to enjoy her touch. Without a doubt, she'd enjoyed his tender exploration of her body, drawing gasping breaths from her and a passion she didn't know existed. She pulled the cover up over her head to hide the blush. She was grateful he was freer than he had been about kissing her and showing affection without freezing up.

A heavy thump landed on her rear. "Get up, woman. I want a good breakfast before we board the train." Cold air hit her exposed feet and legs as the covers were yanked off, and Sam walloped her again with the pillow.

Screeching, she leapt from the bed, cushion in hand, ready to swing at Sam's head. He caught the pillow with one hand and wrapped his other arm around her middle. He tossed the pillow back on the bed and pulled her in for a quick kiss, then swatted her on the behind. "I'm starving. You've got fifteen minutes to get ready."

Aileen peeked out the window and groaned. "It's not even light yet. Why don't you go on down to the dining room, and I'll be down soon."

"All right. Be sure to put your pistol in your reticule or pocket."

"Yes, dear. I will, though I don't think the little bit of practice I had yesterday qualifies me to have it on my person."

He chuckled and tweaked her nose. "Me either. It's just for an emergency...and please...make sure I'm behind you when you fire."

She swatted him on the belly. "I wasn't that bad." His stomach growled. "Go on with you, now, and put some food in that stomach of yours."

They'd packed everything last night, so it didn't take her long to wash and slip into fresh pantalets and a camisole. Sam told her to forget about even trying to put on a corset, as it was getting hot, and she'd be miserable. Going without one would take some getting used to. She put on the shirtwaist blouse and a russet brown serge skirt. They'd bought a holster for her revolver, and her new coat hid it so that, from the front, folks would think she wore a pretty leather belt.

Oh, she loved the boots. They were so comfortable. She left her hat on the bed and went downstairs to join Sam. He stood as she walked in and held her chair. "You are lovely in your new duds. Your new hat will be perfect with the color of your skirt."

"You mean my cowboy hat?"

"No. The one with the big feather"—he fluttered his hand by his head—"on the side."

She giggled. "It's called a plume."

"Yeah, that's it."

"I thought I'd wear my cowboy hat today."

"Actually, it's for home—to keep the sun off your face and neck."

Oh, yes, he'd explained how the sun could be harsh and to prevent burns she needed to stay covered. She did buy several pairs of gloves—one for working in the garden, a pair for horseback riding, and a pair for church. At home in Ireland, they treasured the sunny days, and she didn't know of anyone burned by the sun's rays there.

Their waiter brought their food. Sam had ordered eggs, bacon, ham, biscuits, fried potatoes, and gravy. There was no way she could eat everything on her plate. She peeked up at Sam and cocked an eyebrow.

"Don't worry. What you can't eat I'll finish for you."

He opened his biscuits, slathered gravy all over the tops, and liberally added salt and pepper before taking a bite. She decided to give it a try. Sam surveyed her as she took a bite and waited for a response. "It's bland, but good."

"Try a little salt and pepper. It makes a big difference." She did as he said, and though the flavor was some better, the concoction was definitely an acquired taste.

****

Their train left Abilene at ten a.m. By the time the train stopped to take on coal and water, they'd arrive in Odessa around ten p.m., if nothing unforeseen happened. They'd have a two-hour layover and would arrive in Monahans in early morning. It wouldn't be a comfortable night.

Aileen tapped on the window. "Look, Sam. There's a man standing by the tracks. Will the train stop?" She clutched his arm. "You don't think he could be a train robber, do you?"

Sam leaned over to look. "With those two suitcases, I doubt he's a robber." He nodded toward a cloud of dust. "That's probably his ride heading back home." It didn't happen often, as most folks would at least make it to one of the coal or water stations, but here in West Texas, a man could ride all day and never spot another soul.

They stopped and within five minutes were underway again.

"I'm getting a little nervous. What if Tad doesn't like me?" She twisted her hands in her lap. Sam took one, placed it on his thigh, and intertwined their fingers.

"He'll love you, sweetheart. At first he may be a little obstinate, as he's partial to Ruth, but he'll adapt quickly enough."

"How about you, Sam? What does Ruth mean to you?"

Chapter Ten

Sam dreaded the last leg of their journey—their trip from Monahans to Fort Stockton on the stage would be grueling for Aileen. If the carriage were full, it wouldn't be comfortable, especially for a woman like Aileen. He'd not heard her complain once, so far, but travel on the train was easy compared to that on the stage. She was a genteel lady and not accustomed to the harshness of the barren countryside. Jane hadn't been either, and she'd tried not to complain, but on occasion she had broken down in tears of frustration—when a sandstorm ruined her fresh wash and coated every surface in the house, for instance. No doubt he'd learn how resilient Aileen was to the trials she'd face in her new home.

His heart thumped with happiness at the thought of Tad's excitement when he saw the buckboard approach—jumping up and down and waving his hat in the air. Sam grinned and hugged Aileen closer to him on the seat.

"You're excited to see your son, aren't you? I can scarce contain my joy, and I don't even know the boy."

Her pleasure pleased Sam. He had no doubt as to her sincerity, and she would manage Tad as well as she had Avery Jamison's twin boys.

"How do you think he will react to you bringing home a wife?"

Sam wondered himself. "He'll most likely have mixed emotions for a while, but in time he'll accept and love you." He cleared his throat and mulled over mentioning Ruth again. "He's wanted a ma for a long time…wanted me to marry Ruth."

She frowned and tightened her lips. "Who *is* Ruth? You mentioned her name once before but didn't explain what role she played in your home. Is there any reason she'd think you'd marry her?"

"None other than being Jane's cousin. She came to help out for Tad's birth and never went home. She stayed with us while Jane lived and for a time after she passed. Tad and I wouldn't have survived our grief without her support. And Tad is crazy about her. She's staying with Tad now while I'm gone."

"Didn't the community disapprove of a young unmarried woman living with you?"

"At the time, Rosa wasn't wed and lived in with us, and they shared a room. When Rosa and Miguel married, I found a family that welcomed Ruth into their home. She looks after their two children." For all the good she'd been for them, she'd also been a lot of trouble…to him emotionally. He knew she was in love with him, but he didn't return the sentiment.

"You don't think she'll want to move back in now that you've wed, do you?"

Sam shook his head. "I'll not let that happen."

"Is she in love with you?"

"How the heck am I supposed to know the answer to that?"

"I'm sure you have a pretty good idea. Is she?"

"Yeah, I guess so."

"Why haven't you married her?"

"Darn it, Aileen, where is this conversation going?" He removed his arm from around her shoulders and clenched his hands on his knees.

"Just answer the simple question, Sam."

"Because I didn't love her, that's why."

Big tears pooled in her eyes, and her chin quivered. "But you married me...and...and you don't love me, either."

****

Sam stood. "I'll be in the gentlemen's lounge if you need me." He didn't wait for her answer but strode on down the car.

Aileen wiped at the errant tear on her cheek and struggled to focus her attention elsewhere. She withdrew her embroidery from her reticule. The project, her initials on a handkerchief, being small, easily fit inside the bag. In one corner of the delicate linen fabric, she'd embroidered her initials—A, C, L, and W—with periwinkle blue thread. To add balance, she had placed green shamrocks between the four letters. Around the monogram she'd stitched a garland of delicate flowers and leaves. Today she'd make a dainty rolled hem. And possibly later she could crochet a delicate trim around the entire edge.

The sound of the car door opening drew Aileen's gaze up to observe her husband striding toward her. Determined not to be a pouting wife, she gave him a smile of welcome. "Why back so soon?"

He slid in beside her. "Too smoky in there."

She sniffed. "I can tell. I'm glad you don't smoke." She shuddered. "And I'm glad you don't chew that disgusting tobacco or dip snuff."

"Never cared for any form of tobacco." Sam

slipped out of his jacket and stood. "Let me see if George can find a place to air my coat." He wasn't gone long. "It should smell nice enough to wear by dinner. He had an entire rack of jackets. Guess I'm not the only one who dislikes the aroma."

"Do they drink alcohol in the men's car?"

"Some do, but I've never seen anyone drunk." He glanced down and noticed her questioning gaze. "And no, I don't imbibe very often, and only one or two drinks when I do." Aileen breathed a sigh of relief. She didn't mind the use of alcohol in moderation, but she'd seen some of her father's friends drunk enough times to despise the condition. "I do use alcohol on occasion when performing a procedure on a patient that needs a little numbing but doesn't warrant an anesthetic." His grin wicked, he added, "And if my hand is shaking, I take a dose to help steady my hand."

The day passed slowly. Sam had the newspapers he'd collected at each stop. In Abilene, she'd picked up a copy of *The Ladies' Home Journal* and spent time each day perusing the articles. The crochet doily patterns were a bonus. She'd found thread and hooks at J. W. Reds' Dry Goods Store, where she'd bought clothes, and she spent time each day working on a new pattern. When she held her work up for Sam to admire, he chuckled and said, "Can't picture that frilly scarf on the back of our sofa."

"Why? What's it like?"

"It's constructed of rough hewn timber, with pillows on the seat and back to make it comfortable."

"Hmm, maybe it's time for a new one." His description was hard for her to envisage.

"It looks quite nice on the red clay tiles, with rugs

here and there, but if you want a new one, that's fine. Just nothing too fussy. I like to be comfortable when I sit down."

"I'll withhold judgment until I look at the couch." They spent the next hour discussing the pieces of furniture in their home. Aileen wouldn't try to change things right away, if at all. Her first duty was to gain Tad's friendship and trust...and Rosa's. She didn't know quite what to make of the situation with Ruth. Would the woman resent Aileen? Of course she would, but would she act on her animosity? Aileen didn't want jealousy to prevent a possible friendship, but she had to make it clear...*she* was Sam's wife.

After the evening meal and several cups of coffee, they made sure their luggage was ready to be unloaded when they arrived in Monahans. Sam urged her to put on the most comfortable dress she owned and her new jacket. The revolver was to be tucked into a pocket, not displayed on her hip, and she could wear her cowboy hat.

"The stage usually arrives at seven thirty a.m. and departs at eight a.m. There is a cafe close to the depot where we can grab breakfast. I wouldn't drink too much tea, if I were you, as privacy breaks will be few and far between."

"But what if you *really* have to go...bad?"

A grimace distorted Sam's face. She feared he was in pain and clutched his arm to have him burst out in loud guffaws. People in the car turned to look at them, big grins on their faces, and they didn't even know why Sam was laughing. When he could control his outburst, he bent down to whisper in her ear, "Why, you either hold it or use the chamber pot stored under the seat."

Aileen's jaw dropped. It must have, or at least her expression must have aped her horror, as Sam burst into a paroxysm of chuckles. She swatted him on the arm. "You're teasing me! And folks are staring at us." She eyed him as he regained control. "You are joking, aren't you?"

"Yes." He pulled her close and kissed her forehead. With her head on his chest, she heard the rumbles of his laughter. "Though I did read of a king in Europe who had his chamber pot in his carriage and used it often, regardless of who was in attendance."

"I wouldn't doubt that, but even if there were a vessel in the coach, I'd not use it."

"Don't worry. We'll stop probably every twelve miles to change the mules and have ten minutes to tend to nature's call."

"How far will we be traveling?"

"It's fifty miles from Monahans to Fort Stockton. If we can make eight miles an hour, which is an optimistic estimate, we should make it home by two or three in the afternoon." That didn't sound so bad to Aileen. "It all depends on who is driving and the condition of the road. As soon as we arrive, I'll get the buckboard while you stay with the luggage."

"Will it take very long to get home then?" She hoped it'd still be light so she could view her new home. He'd said it was dry, barren country, but at times of the year the cactus bloomed and painted the desert in watercolor hues.

"We're only a mile or so outside of town, no more than an hour, usually less." His large hand massaged her neck, and she sat forward to give him better access. "If you keep that up, I'll fall asleep right here."

"When George makes up the beds tonight, we need to turn in early and try to sleep, if possible. We'll stay dressed, so we'll be ready to disembark as soon as the train stops. It won't stay long in Monahans before heading west."

Aileen thought she'd toss and turn all night, but once she got comfortable, the soft rumble of Sam's snoring lulled her, and she drifted.

****

They'd just finished breakfast in the cafe next to the depot and returned from the outhouse when the stage roared in and stopped in front of the stand, sending dust flying. Aileen watched in fascination as a gate swung open and the six mules and stagecoach entered. In ten minutes, the coach came out the same door with fresh stock and a different driver. She'd like to glimpse the inside, but the tender called out, "If you're traveling to Fort Stockton, pay up. First come, first served."

Sam took her arm and hustled her over to the man. "I want two seats facing the front." He counted out a number of bills.

"Claim your seats, mister."

Sam helped her inside. She sat in the middle of the front-facing seat, and he took the one to her right, by the door. A man in a military uniform took the seat on her left. An older couple and a cowboy sat down across from them. Seven men still stood around the tender.

"Any of you men interested in the center seat?" Several stepped forward and paid their money. "The rest of you'll ride on top. You can switch out with the center seat 'bout halfway there."

Thank goodness they didn't have to bump knees

with those three men. Plus the middle bench had a makeshift backrest—a wide piece of cut leather stretched and attached from one side to the other. Pieces of leather dangled from the ceiling. Aileen shot Sam a questioning glance. "Those in the center hold on to steady themselves when the road is rough." He pulled her arm under his and laid her hand on his bicep. "We'll get more dust on this row, but traveling backwards makes some folks sick." He leaned down and whispered in her ear. "Plus, I didn't want you interlocking your knees with the center row."

Aileen felt sorry for the elderly lady, but not enough to offer to trade places.

The station tender stood at the open door. "All right, folks. Remember, no shooting out the windows unless it's in defense. If you don't follow the rules, the driver will put you off in the desert. He's done it before. Men, be respectful of the ladies." He slammed the door.

Sam squeezed her hand. "Hang on."

She heard the crack of a whip and the driver's bellow, "Go, boys!" The coach leapt forward, and Aileen's head bounced against the back wall. Thank goodness it was padded.

Sam caught Aileen to steady her and prevent further jostling until the coach settled into a steady gait. He chuckled as she repositioned her hat. "You all right?"

"I'm fine. You said he'd take off like a shot, but I assumed you were exaggerating."

The lady across the way eyed Aileen with distaste. Sam noticed she listened in on his and Aileen's conversation, and then said something to her husband. He frowned and muttered, "Mind your own business,

Ethel."

Ethel studied Aileen from head to toe, well, as much of her toes as she could observe. Aileen wore one of her new dresses—blue cotton, but it was thick enough for winter wear. He'd cautioned her to wear something comfortable. Over the dress, she wore her new jacket, which she could take off if the day grew too hot. Ethel wore a suit dress of heavy gray wool and appeared to be fully corseted. She'd already removed the matching cape and placed it on her knees. Sam hadn't purchased a blanket, as he didn't believe the weather would warrant the need for one. With any luck, he'd not made a mistake.

Ethel made up her mind. She lifted her chin, sniffed, and asked, "Where you from, young woman? Sounds like you have one of them Irish accents."

"It is Irish. I've only been in the States for three months." She smiled up at Sam. "We've been wed just a little over a week."

The matron snorted. "Come over to get you a rich husband, huh?"

Her husband bit out, "Ethel, for God's sake, woman! Shut your mouth."

Aileen's face reddened, and she sat up straighter. "Ethel, not that it's any of your concern, but I didn't have to marry for money. I admire Dr. Walker."

Sam had difficulty keeping his anger in check. The old biddy had no right to insult Aileen. He leaned down and kissed her hair, and then glanced back at Ethel. "As a matter of fact, madam, my wife is an heiress." He winked at Aileen. "I'm the one who married for money."

The three cowboys in the center roared with

laughter. One slapped his knees as he hooted, "Har, har, har." He turned back and tipped his hat. "Good for you, old man. Looks like you got a beauty in the bargain."

Aileen blushed scarlet. Sam slipped his arm around her shoulders and worked it down to her waist. He snuggled her closer. "I did indeed, sir."

"I'm Johnson." The one who'd spoken swiveled around and offered his hand. He pointed to his companions. "This here's Dickens and Smith." He pointed to the wrangler by Ethel. "That be Oats." Sam shook Johnson's hand, thumped the brim of his hat, and nodded to the others. "Pleased to meet you. I'm Samuel Walker, and this is my wife." They all four tipped their hats and mumbled, "Ma'am." The two with their back to her had to twist their necks.

Sam leaned forward and turned to the soldier. "How about you, Lieutenant?"

"Jeremy Hawkins, sir." He offered his hand. "You are Captain Walker, are you not?"

He didn't recognize the young man, but time on the prairie changed a person. "I am, or was, but I'm sorry I don't remember you."

"No reason to. I was fortunate enough to stay away from your domain, but I saw you around from time to time."

"Frank Hardy, gentlemen, ma'am. As you've surmised, this is my wife, Ethel. She can be quite nice when you get used to her ways."

Ethel snorted and shot daggers at her husband. He merely patted her knee. His belly bobbed up and down with his silent chuckles. Sam glanced at Aileen. Her eyes were round as saucers, and she'd caught her bottom lip with her teeth. He supposed it was to keep from giggling.

Sam pointed out the window. "Do you see those plants with the long green stalks and red flowers on the top?"

She peered around him. There were a number of them growing amid the prickly pear cactus, creosote bushes, and buffalo grass, names she'd learned when they'd neared Abilene and Monahans. "Yes, I see them." She tilted her head. "I guess they could be pretty, with the right backdrop."

"Wait until you see a field full of them in bloom at sunset. It resembles a sea of red." She leaned back in the seat.

"I'd like that. Do they bloom all the time?"

"No, usually around this time of year—March through April—depending on the amount of rain we get. You can break one of the long stalks off and plant it in the ground. Eventually, with time and care, you can have a living, blooming fence." He lifted one of her hands and examined the soft pads of her fingers. "You must be careful though, as behind each little green leaf is a thorn. Always wear thick gloves."

She looked around and scrunched up her nose. "What is that smell?"

All three men on the middle seat chimed, "Oats!"

The young man blushed scarlet and blurted, "It weren't me." He kicked the shin of the wrangler across from him.

"Yeow! Darn it, that hurt."

Johnson added, "Ma'am, please excuse Oats. He didn't have a mama to teach him manners."

Wide-eyed and red-faced, Aileen turned to Sam. "I'm talking about that stinky medicine smell."

Silence reigned. Sam struggled to keep a straight face. Hardy didn't even try. He slapped his leg and howled, "Har-d-har-har-har." Everyone else in the coach joined him, even Ethel. Aileen gazed around in confusion, but finally chuckled with them.

She sobered. "I don't appreciate being the butt of jokes"—she threw her hands up—"especially when I don't have a clue what you're talking about."

"Aw, ma'am, we weren't laughing at you. We thought Oats had…well, uh-hum…you know."

When she didn't respond, Sam leaned close to her and whispered, "They thought someone had passed gas and that was the odor you were smelling."

She stiffened and murmured, "Gosh, why would I draw attention to such?"

"Well, anyways, I think what you're smelling is the old ugly creosote bush." Johnson pointed out his side of the coach. "See the small bush with the little yellow flowers and green leaves?"

She nodded.

"They stink so bad the cattle won't eat them 'less they're starving, but I'm told the Indians make medicine from the shrub." He looked to Sam for confirmation.

"That's right, they do. They dry the leaves and stems, crush them, and then boil them to make a tea used for a variety of ailments. The mixture can also be made into a paste to treat conditions of the skin."

"And, Dr. Walker, do you make use of these concoctions in treating your patients?" asked Mrs. Hardy.

"No, ma'am, I do not, but only because I don't know enough about them. I hope one day to be able to visit one of the Indian medicine men in the area and learn."

"Harrumph. You'd trust anything those heathens told you about healing?"

"Yes, ma'am, I would—especially if out in the middle of nowhere without medical supplies. I'd say their teachings would be invaluable."

****

Ten minutes wasn't nearly long enough for Aileen. She'd visited one of the outhouses, washed her hands and face, and was helped back into the stage. Her muscles still screamed for a walk to loosen the tension. This time when the driver cracked his whip she was ready, and though the motion threw her back a little, she didn't hit her head.

The same cowboys boarded and occupied the center seat. Evidently the ones on top liked their spot and were not willing to trade. They each held a bundle, and the minute the coach was underway, they started eating biscuits.

Aileen reached for her reticule and lifted out the parcel the cook at the cafe in Monahans had put together for them. Wrapped in heavy butcher paper, its oils hadn't soaked through to her personal items. She removed the string and folded the edges of the paper back. "Sam, take your pick. I'm afraid if I lift the parcel, I'll spill the food everywhere." He selected one oozing with butter and apricot jam. "Eating your dessert first, huh?"

He winked. "You bet. I've always had a sweet tooth."

She giggled and picked up a biscuit. The sugary marmalade oozed from the side, and she licked it off to keep it from dropping. To their left, the lieutenant wasn't eating. She swallowed the bite she had in her mouth. "Lieutenant, could we offer you a biscuit? We've plenty."

He gazed down at her lap. "You sure?"

"I'm positive. Take two. Sam bought extra just in case someone had forgotten to bring something."

"Go ahead, Hawkins," said Sam. "If you don't, I'll eat more than I should, and suffer the remainder of the trip."

"Thank you, ma'am. Much obliged." He lifted two biscuits. "I would've gotten grub here, but last trip the bread was wormy."

The cowboys stilled. All looked down, studied their biscuits, and then went back to eating.

"Mr. and Mrs. Hardy, do you have food over there?"

"Yes, dear, we do, and that's mighty nice of you to ask." She tried to look around the men in front of her to see if Ethel had truly spoken. The woman caught Aileen peeping, smiled, and nodded. Strange, coming from the woman who'd been so rude this morning.

When there were four biscuits remaining, Sam folded the paper around the greatly reduced package and tied the strings. "We may get hungry on the way home this afternoon."

She tucked the bundle back in her bag.

Home...they were almost home. She couldn't believe they'd come so far in so little time. They'd been traveling nine days and spent two nights in Abilene. She rested her head against Sam's shoulder and watched as the desert landscape flew by. Occasionally, they'd glimpse low mountains in the background, but mostly just flat land with more creosote bushes, mesquite trees, cacti, and prairie grass. They'd passed all the ocotillo they'd catch sight of for a while, but Sam assured her she'd see more. Blue flowers grew among the other plants, especially along the trail. Sam said they were lupine, better known in Texas as bluebonnets.

She dozed off and on. The wheels hitting holes and ruts in the road jolted her awake. The rolling motion of the carriage rocked her back to sleep. When the driver's horn sounded to announce their arrival to the stage tender, she sat up and gazed around at their surroundings. They were home—dirt, adobe buildings, cacti, and a few trees. Sam had said Fort Stockton wasn't much of a town and had little foliage. The colors of the buildings, bleached by the sun, were pale, as were the couple of trees obscured in dust. The scene resembled a black-and-white painting.

Chapter Eleven

Sam jumped down from the stage and turned to help Aileen. She appeared dazed as she gazed around at what little there was to see in Fort Stockton. He'd told her it was desolate, and by golly, he didn't want to hear any griping.

She folded her arm around his and smiled up at him. "Glory be, you were right. There is no' much around. Ach, we'll be having to entertain ourselves, then."

The tension in Sam's chest eased. He pulled her close for a hug. "That we will, my dear." He led her around to the other side of the coach. Comanche Springs lay before them, the clear cool water providing nourishment for the bordering grass and trees.

"Oh, 'tis lovely."

As passengers disembarked from the stage, onlookers flowed from Kruger's store, the attached saloon, and the gambling house to gape at the newcomers. He gazed down the street, and sure enough, a few cowboys drifted their way from the only other saloon in town.

A wagon pulled by two mules drove up and stopped along the bank of the springs. Tom Smithson set the brake. His wife, Suzy, jumped down and squealed, "Mama, Mama, you made it." She reached her mother and held Ethel in a tight grip. Mrs. Hardy pretended to fuss as she adjusted her clothing when released, but her actions didn't fool a soul. She removed a hanky from her pocket and turned to blow her nose. Mr. Hardy watched their exchange and then opened his arms. "Suzy, you have a squeeze for your old man?" She flew into his embrace. "Daddy, I'm so glad to see you and Mama."

He patted her back, and if Sam weren't mistaken, a tear glistened in the older man's eye. "We've missed you, pumpkin." He eyed her husband, Tom, and nodded before turning back to his daughter. "Tom been treating you right?"

She rushed to her husband's side. "Oh, Daddy, of course he has."

Hardy muttered, "Better be, else I'll be..."

Ethel took Suzy's arm and led her over to Aileen. "Daughter, this is Aileen Walker, wife to the good doctor here." She lowered her voice and muttered, "She's Irish, but don't hold that against her. She's a good girl."

Suzy rolled her eyes and slipped her arm under Aileen's. "Welcome to Fort Stockton, Mrs. Walker. I'm Suzy Smithson." She waved to the men. "And that handsome fella is my husband, Tom. We've known Dr. Walker for some time. I hope we'll be able to get together often. We need more women in this town."

"Please, call me Aileen. It will take a little while for me to settle in, but as soon as I do, I'll call on you."

"Hey, Dr. Walker, help me with this trunk." The driver stood on top of the stage and lifted the trunk down to Sam.

He hoisted the chest to his shoulder and turned to the Hardys. "Will you keep Aileen company while I put this in the buckboard?"

"We'd be pleased to, Sam." Hardy slapped him on the shoulder. "Go on and take care of business. I'm anxious to walk around and work some of the kinks out of my joints."

Sam winked at Aileen. "Be right back, sweetheart."

The owner of the blacksmith shop and stable had Sam's wagon hitched and waiting down the street. He eased the trunk into the back. "Appreciate it, Johnson. I'll be back in a few minutes to settle up."

"Take your time, Sam." He was pleased to know the Hardys were keeping an eye on Aileen. Though Fort Stockton was peaceful most of the time, the cowboys could be obnoxious when a new woman hit town, though strangely enough at the dances and parties they didn't get out of hand. He pulled the buckboard up behind the coach and stopped. Hopefully Mr. Kruger had his supplies ready to load.

He hopped down from the wagon to collect Aileen. "Mr. and Mrs. Hardy, I hope we see you again while you're here." He shook hands with Tom. "You and Suzy also."

"We'll plan on it," said Suzy.

Sam escorted Aileen into the store. "Mr. Kruger, I'd like to introduce you to my wife. She may come in on her own and need to charge things to our account."

Mr. Kruger wiped his hands on his apron. "Mrs. Walker, ma'am, it's a pleasure to meet you." He shook her hand and then turned. "Martha, come say hello to Sam's wife." Aileen started at his yell.

Martha waddled from the back room, her face aglow with a smile. She caught Sam in her arms and hugged. Sam had learned to embrace back. It was the only way the woman would turn loose. Sam laughed. "Meet my wife, Martha." She turned to Aileen, took both of her hands, and studied her from head to toe as he said, "Aileen, this is Martha Kruger. If you're not careful, she'll hug you to death."

Aileen laughed. "Ach, I love a good cuddle myself." She threw her arms around the older woman. "Pleased to make your acquaintance, Mrs. Kruger." She nodded to Mr. Kruger. "And you also, sir."

Martha laughed. "Now, this young woman has been raised right. She's a hugger. Call me Martha, dear." She elbowed Sam. "You got yourself an Irish lass, Sam. Good for you." She patted Aileen's hand. "Come visit me one morning after you get settled, and we'll share a pot of tea."

"I'll make sure she gets here, Martha, but we need to head home and see my boy." Adrenaline rushed through his body at the thought.

"Of course you're anxious, son. 'Spect he's grown a couple of inches while you've been gone."

Sam was afraid of that very thing. He didn't like to miss out on Tad's growth and progress. He and Herman Kruger had Sam's supplies loaded in short time. The older man turned to go back inside. "Herman, can I speak with you a minute?" Sam motioned with his head, and they strolled off a short distance from the others.

"Why, sure. What's on your mind?"

He glanced around to make sure no one paid them any attention. "Aileen left Ireland under stressful circumstances. It's possible her father and an associate of his will be looking for her. I don't want them to know she's here."

117

Herman arched a brow. "Do they mean to do her harm?"

"Not necessarily harm, but disrupt her happiness."

"Her own father?" Herman shook his head. "Does she want him to find her?"

"No. He has gambling debts and wants her money."

The older man spit on the ground. "Don't worry, Sam. I'll keep my yap shut and tell Martha to do the same."

"Thanks, friend." Herman walked off shaking his head, and Sam strode to the front of the buckboard. "Aileen, do you need anything before we go?"

"Not that I know of. I'll have to get settled first. Oh, wait, do we have tea?"

"I expect we do."

Martha appeared with a small wooden box in her arms. She handed it to Aileen. "A little wedding gift from us."

Sam took the box so Aileen could lift the lid. Inside, tucked in straw, lay a china teapot with four cups and matching saucers. Aileen lifted one of the cups and studied the pattern. Tears pooled in her eyes as she gazed up at Sam.

"Look, 'tis Irish china. See the little clovers?" She carefully positioned the cup back in the straw and turned to Martha. "'Tis lovely, ma'am." She placed her arms around the older woman and squeaked out, "Thank you so much. I'll cherish it always."

Martha patted her on the back. "Now, now, dear…no tears. I wanted you to have it because I know how much it would mean to you." She pulled back from Aileen and patted her cheek. "Now, enjoy."

Aileen turned to Herman. Before he knew what was happening, she'd wrapped him in a hug. "Thank you also, Mr. Kruger."

He blustered, clearly shaken by the embrace, but by the expression on his face, he was pleased. "Well, now...you're welcome, young woman." Taking Martha's arm, he mumbled, "Where'd that come from?"

"From the bunch Mrs. Whitaker ordered. That uppity woman stuck us with a whole set of the dishes after she hightailed it back to Abilene." Sam couldn't help but overhear their conversation as he helped Aileen onto the seat of the wagon. "I knew just the right person would come along and want it. May even be able to sell the entire batch."

****

Aileen held on to the seat of the wagon as Sam prodded the mules into motion. "We live west of town about a mile. Shouldn't take us long to get there."

"I'm glad it's not dark yet. I want to be able to distinguish where we're going so I can find my way back."

As they left town, the road roughened, and Aileen found herself bouncing on the hard wooden seat. She giggled. "I may have to make a pad for this seat. I'll be bruised by the time we reach home."

Sam laughed. "You'll get used to it, but if you intend to make a cushion, make it out of something the weather won't hurt." He thought a minute. "I'll see if I can find a piece of cowhide big enough."

"Thank you."

The wagon kicked up dirt. Fortunately, it whipped back behind them. Regardless, she'd have an extra layer when they got home. Her stomach growled. She opened her reticule and withdrew the package of biscuits. "Can you eat and guide the mules at the same time?"

"You bet." Sam switched both pairs of reins to his left hand, and she placed a bacon biscuit in his right. He took a big bite. "Hmm...good. I was starving."

"Me too." She took a big bite. Butter and apricot jelly oozed from it, and she raced to catch all the dribbles with her tongue. Sam watched with interest. "Did I get it all?"

"There's one little bit of jelly"—he bent his head to hers—"right here." His tongue raked her lower lip and she jumped, but stilled when he replaced his tongue with his lips. "Mmm, delicious. I don't believe I've had a kiss all day."

She pulled him back and pressed her lips to his. "Well, we can't have you missing your daily requirement." She handed him another biscuit and started on the last one. After chewing and swallowing a bite, she asked, "What is your quota, anyway?"

He stuffed the last morsel of his food into his mouth, put his arm around her, and pulled her closer to him. "Why, as many as I want, sweetheart."

They hit a large rut and both bounced in the air. "Oh, my china!" She looked behind them, but everything appeared intact.

"It's packed well to prevent breakage."

Aileen's heart sang. Her husband enjoyed her company, and she relished his. Hopefully, when they arrived home, Tad would learn to like and accept her. She sighed, linked her arm with Sam's, and squeezed. "I'm so happy."

"Me too, sweetheart." He kissed her forehead and

nodded. "Look up ahead. There's the house, with the barn and corral out back." He grinned. "I wish I had a horn like the stage drivers, to announce our arrival."

"Oh, I imagine your boy will hear these wheels rattling down the road and come running."

"Yeah, you're right." He looked at the sky. Twilight was falling. "I'm glad we'll arrive before dark." He lifted his pocket watch from his vest pocket and held it to catch the remaining sunlight. "It's almost seven o'clock. With any luck, Tad won't be in bed asleep."

"I'm sure when he hears your voice, he'll wake. It won't hurt for him to be up late on such a special occasion."

Sam squeezed her waist. "I agree. Of course, it may take forever to settle him down."

Aileen studied the house as they drew closer. Made of adobe, it spread long and low across the almost barren land. Several cacti of different varieties grew around the yard. A few were blooming. One tree grew at the front, providing shade to cool the breeze as it passed through to the house.

Sam removed his arm from around her waist and spurred the mules into a faster gait. The screen door slammed, and a young boy, barefooted and with his nightshirt slapping his legs, ran out into the road, yelling, "Pa, Pa...you're home!"

A young, dark-haired woman ran after him. "Don't get in the road."

He stopped at the edge, but jumped up and down, yelling, "Pa, Pa, Pa!"

"Is that Ruth?"

"Yes, it is."

"Whoa, boys." He stopped the mules, secured the brake, reached down, and lifted Tad into his lap. Sam clasped the boy close. "I've missed you, son." Feeling the boy's feet, he muttered, "You'll catch a cold running around barefooted."

"I was plum excited and forgot my shoes."

Sam waved to the woman in the yard. "He's fine, Ruth. I'll let him stay up with us a little longer."

She waved, but turned and strode to the house.

Sam set Tad on the seat between them.

Tad glanced at Aileen. "Hi, lady. What's your name?"

She offered Tad her hand. He glanced at it and then to her before taking it and shaking. "Hello, young man. My name is Aileen. I've heard so much about you."

His eyes rounded. "Really?" He leaned toward Sam. "You talk funny."

"That's rude, son."

"'Tis okay, Sam. It's only natural to notice my accent is different."

Sam clicked the reins. "Gee, boys." The animals veered left into the yard. At "Haw," they swung right and moved toward the barn.

A Mexican man came from the outbuilding. "Hey, Doctor Sam. It's good you are home." His gaze studied Aileen before he doffed his hat and nodded.

"Thanks, Miguel. I'm pleased to be here."

Sam set the brake, hopped down, and reached for Tad. He set the boy on his feet and turned to help Aileen descend from the wagon. Arm around her waist, he led her to the man holding the reins of the mules, ready to lead them into the barn. "Miguel, this is my wife…Aileen Lynch Walker."

Miguel whipped his hat from his head, held it against his heart, and made a quick bow. "*Señora*, I am honored to meet you."

"You also, Miguel."

He grinned at Sam. "Congratulations, *Señor*. Rosa will be so pleased you'll not be alone." He slapped his hat back on his head. "Are you hungry? Shall I have Rosa fix you something?"

"Don't bother her. We'll find something to hold us over until morning. Soon as you finish in the barn, you can head home. I'll unload supplies tomorrow."

Sam put a hand to Aileen's back to direct her into the house. Tad skipped along beside them. "This is the courtyard. In the summer vines cover the top and provide a little respite from the hot sun."

"It must be beautiful." The floor was a brick tile of some type, which no doubt made it easier to keep clean. They entered the house through a pair of double glass doors into a large room with the same tile on the floor. A fireplace covered the wall on one end of the room, the opposite end served as a dining room, and past that wall was the kitchen. "'Tis lovely, Sam."

"I like it. When the temperature is really hot, we can open doors on both sides of the room for airflow. Each of the bedrooms, except Tad's, have doors to the terrace." He walked to a door off the dining room and called, "Ruth?"

"She's been stayin' in your bedroom, Pa, so she could be closer to me." He whispered, "I think she gots scared."

Sam walked to the hallway by the fireplace. "Ruth, come out a minute, please. I want you to meet someone."

"I'm coming. Just a minute." When the woman entered the room, she had an armful of clothes and personal belongings. She dropped them on the sofa, walked to Sam, and embraced him. "I'm so glad you're home. We've missed you."

Aileen studied the young woman, who was probably no more than five years older than herself. Her calico dress emphasized an ample figure, and the blue brought out the color of her eyes. Her dark hair, brushed to a sheen, gleamed in the glow of the kerosene lamps.

Forehead furrowed, Sam placed his hands on her shoulders and set her away from him but didn't release her. He turned her toward Aileen. "Ruth, this is my wife, Aileen. We were married in Boston the day before we boarded the train."

"Married...?" Her partial smile turned ugly.

"Hello, Ruth. Sam has told me a lot about you and your cousin Jane. I'm pleased to make your acquaintance at last." She offered a hand to the woman. Ruth stared at it for what seemed like five minutes but in truth was a couple of seconds, but she never took it. She smiled, but the expression was the most evil smile Aileen had ever seen. This woman hated her. She'd best be on her toes.

"Welcome. I'm sure you'll be happy here." She snatched her clothes off the sofa and left the room without a backward glance.

Tad pulled on Sam's jacket. "Pa, Aunt Rufe wanted to be my ma." He glared at Aileen and yelled, "I don't want you for my ma. Go away."

Sam snatched the boy up in his arms. "That's enough, young man. I'll explain it all tomorrow, but you must be nice to Aileen. I'd hate to have to punish you as soon as I got home."

Chapter Twelve

Tired as she was, Aileen couldn't sleep. Sam's big bed cocooned her in comfort, easing her mind. His soft snores should have helped her drift off, but something niggled at her awareness—probably Ruth's evil stare. Aileen feared the woman would be trouble, and had told Sam as much before bed. He promised to take her home tomorrow.

She lay on Sam's arm, and as she turned to face him, she eased her arm across his chest. In his sleep, he stroked it with his free hand. The tender caress calmed her, and she closed her eyes.

A sound outside the patio door startled her…soft scraping…probably just a small animal. The door was closed, as the nights were cool in the desert. At a tap on the glass, she jerked up to a sitting position. Ruth stood outside peering in at them. Aileen shook Sam.

"What…what is it?"

"Ruth is outside spying on us."

Sam lurched from the bed just as Ruth turned and ran. He yanked the curtains closed. Back in bed, he pulled her close and whispered against her hair, "Don't worry. She'll be gone after breakfast."

After her fitful night's sleep, Aileen eased from the bed, trying not to wake Sam. Still in her nightgown, water pitcher in hand, she dashed barefoot to the kitchen to retrieve hot water from the reservoir attached to the side of the cast iron stove. Rosa wasn't yet in the kitchen, but coals from the stove had kept the water warm.

Back in the bedroom, Sam was up and pulling on work pants. "Good morning. Did you sleep well?"

Aileen set the water jug on the washstand before speaking. "No, not very. Ruth's appearance spooked me, and I couldn't relax."

"I'm sorry, sweetheart." He cupped her face and pressed a light kiss on her mouth. "Tonight will be better. I promise."

"I certainly don't blame you, Sam, but that woman scares me."

"She's beginning to scare me also." He stepped into his cowboy boots. "I'll light a fire in the fireplace so the living area will warm up." At the door, he stopped and turned. "Save me a little of that water."

Aileen grinned. "Yes, dear."

Aileen entered the living area to see Rosa setting the table. She looked up and smiled. "*Señora*, welcome."

"Thank you, and please, call me Aileen."

"I will try, but…" She smiled. "I cannot promise." She motioned to a chair. "Have a seat, and I will pour you a cup of coffee. Or would you like tea?"

"I'll drink coffee this morning." She walked to one of the glass doors and looked outside. "Where's Sam?"

"He is in the *niño*'s room. He said words about a talk." She walked back into the kitchen.

"Here, let me help. I can't sit while you're working. Besides, I need to stay busy." She dreaded Ruth's appearance at the table. It would be hard for Aileen to keep her mouth shut about last night's visit.

"Miss Ruth does not have trouble being waited on."

Aileen picked up silverware and carried it to the table. "That's not in my nature. Well, although I say that, we did have servants at home, but I was allowed to work in the kitchen at times. Cook taught me to cook many things—how to cut up a chicken, make bread, and a variety of desserts."

"Where are you from, *Señora*? Your talk is different."

"I'm from Ireland. We all talk like this over there." She chuckled. "Your talk is different, too."

Rosa laughed. "*Si, si*, it is. I am learning English, but it is difficult."

"I hope you'll teach me Spanish."

The back door opened, and Miguel walked in carrying a bucket of milk. "Good morning, *Señora*."

"Good morning, Miguel."

He set the pail on the counter. "Tell the *señor* I've hitched the mules to the wagon."

"I will, and thank you."

As he left, Rosa said, "I am curious to find out what you have in that small wooden crate on the sideboard."

"It's a tea set from Ireland, a gift from Mr. and Mr. Kruger at the store." She rushed to the sideboard and pulled the top off the crate. With care, she lifted the glassware from the wood shavings and arranged the tea service to her satisfaction. "Isn't it beautiful?"

"Oh, yes, *Señora*." Rosa touched the rim of one of the delicate saucers. "Would you like to use one of the cups this morning?"

"No, I'll wait for a special occasion."

Tad's door opened, and he walked out dressed for the day, Sam on his heels. Sam eased the boy into the room before turning to go into their bedroom.

"Good morning, Tad."

"Mornin'." Head down, he drew pretend designs on the floor with the toe of his boot. "Pa said I'm to say sorry for bein' rude last night." Aileen waited. She wasn't about to let the little bugger off the hook.

"And?"

His head shot up. "And what?"

"Do I get an apology?"

He drew a deep breath. Aileen struggled not to laugh. "Sorry, ma'am."

"Thank you, Tad. I accept your apology." He shrugged his little shoulders. "You know, it takes a fine young man to be able to say he's sorry."

His expression and demeanor straightened. "Pa said you're my stepmother." He stuck his chin out. "I ain't gonna call you Ma."

"Then I don't think you should. You can call me Aileen, if you like. You know, in Ireland where I'm from, we call our mothers Mam."

"Ha, ha, that's funny...Mam. Sorta like 'yes, ma'am.' "

"Yes, it could mean that; however, in our culture, the word signifies love and respect."

Sam strode from the bedroom. "Breakfast ready? I'm starving."

Rosa bustled in with a large platter of bacon and eggs. "Yes, it is, Doctor Sam. Have a seat, and I will fetch your coffee and the biscuits and gravy."

"I'll bring the coffee." Aileen grabbed a thick cloth to hold around the handle of the large pot and, fearing she'd drop it, held a folded dishtowel to the bottom. She poured the brew into two of the cups. "What about Ruth?"

"She'll want tea. I have water heated."

"Don't bother. She can drink coffee, milk, or water. Where is she, anyway?" Sam stood and walked toward her room. He knocked on the door. "Breakfast is ready and getting cold."

"I'm coming." The door opened, and Ruth preceded Sam from the hallway. "Good morning."

Aileen returned the coffeepot to the stove as a chorus of "good mornings" echoed around the room. When she returned, Sam seated Ruth and waited at the chair to his right to seat Aileen. "Thank you, Sam."

"Tad, would you like to give the blessing this morning?"

"Do I haveta?

"Yes, son, you do."

He folded his hands on the table and squeezed his eyes tight. "Thanks for Rosa's good cooking, Lord, and for Pa and Aunt Ruth and...Aileen." He forced one eyelid up, stabbed Aileen with his stare, and expelled a deep sigh. "I don't want no stepmother...but since I gots one, I'll try to be nice. Please watch over my ma and baby sister up there in heaven. And if you gots time, please send me a dog. Amen."

"Amen." Sam's rumbling voice drowned out the two women's. "That was very nice, Tad." His voice was steady, but he held in his laughter. "You're wanting a dog, huh?"

Tad wiped the milk mustache from his face with the sleeve of his shirt. "Yes, sir, Pa. I'm big enough to take care of one."

"Hmm, I'll give it some thought," he said. "Aileen, your china looks right at home there on the sideboard."

"Ach, yes. I'm so pleased with it, I could bust."

Tad glanced at the cabinet. "Yeah, it's kinda purty. Kinda girly-looking, though."

"Yes, son, it is girly. You're not to touch those, all right?"

"Sure, Pa."

They finished their meal with the occasional chitchat, Tad carrying on most of the conversation.

Finished, Sam stood. "Ruth, if you'll collect your things, I'll drive you into town."

Her jaw dropped. "You're kicking me out today…this morning?"

He blew out a lungful of air. "I'm not kicking you out. Aren't you anxious to return home to your charges?"

"Not really." She stood, shot Aileen a look of pure hatred, and pranced off, the ruffles on her over-exaggerated skirt dancing with her every movement.

"I'll be out front in ten minutes. Be ready."

"Sam, don't forget to give her the gift you brought back from Boston."

"Yeah, Pa, can I have mine now too?"

"No, you may not." He tousled Tad's hair. "You can open it when I get back."

"Yes, sir." Dejected, hands in his pockets, he stalked out the front door.

"I'll see you this afternoon, sweetheart." He tilted her face for his kiss. She clasped his shoulders for balance to return the embrace. "I need to check on a few patients."

"We'll be here."

Aileen helped Rosa clear the table and scraped the food leavings into the scrap bucket. She heard Ruth enter the dining room. Curiosity drove her to step from the kitchen. She'd try to say something nice to the woman before she left.

Ruth stood in front of the buffet, one of the dainty china cups in her hands. She glanced up at Aileen, smiled, and let the piece fall. It shattered, scattering glass across the floor. She covered her mouth to hide her smirk. "Oops!"

Heat suffused Aileen's face and adrenalin forced her to move. She planted her fist in Ruth's face, sending her back against the wall. The next thing she remembered was the pain on her knuckles.

****

Sam walked into the house to witness Aileen's punch that sent Ruth stumbling back. Too stunned to speak, he watched in silence as Ruth wiped her mouth, looked at the blood on her hand, and charged Aileen. Her scream mimicking that of a banshee as she grabbed Aileen's hair with both hands and yanked, pulling Aileen's head forward. Not to be outdone, Aileen reached up and tangled her hands in Ruth's long tresses. She put her head in Ruth's stomach and pushed until the woman smashed into the wall. The back of her head bounced off the adobe.

She loosened her grip on Aileen's hair and slid down the wall, wailing. "You're…crazy. You could've killed me."

"You started this fight, missy. You broke that tea cup a-purpose." Aileen shook her fist. "Don't ever touch anything of mine again, or you'll catch another taste of me fist."

"Sam," Ruth sobbed, her hand stretched out toward him, "it was an accident, I promise."

Aileen swirled to face him. "She's lying. She stood right there, dropped the cup and said, 'Oops.' " Her face red, Aileen swatted at the tear sliding down her cheek. "Believe whomever you want, Sam, but I hope you'll keep her away from me...us. She's evil...obsessed...a demon."

Sam walked to the blubbering woman on the floor and helped her stand. She threw herself into his arms and clutched at his shirt. "Surely you don't believe her over me. Why, we...we've been close for years, and you...you barely know her."

"She's my wife, Ruth. Evidently I don't know you at all." He eased her aside and went to Aileen and encircled her with his arms. "Are you all right, sweetheart?"

"I'm fine. Just angry...and hurt. You know what the tea set means to me."

He stroked her cheek. "I do, and I'm so sorry. We'll order another."

"It's no' the cup but the wickedness of the act." She sneered at Ruth. "She's no longer welcome in our home."

"You can't do that. Why...why...I'm related to Tad. You've no right to keep me from seeing him." She lifted her chin. "Anyhow, this is Sam's home, not yours."

"Ruth, I'll make the final decision after I've learned what ideas you've planted in my son's mind, but until then, Aileen is right. You're not welcome. And this is *our* home." He gathered up her things and slung them over his arm. With the other he grasped Ruth's elbow. "Come along now."

She wrenched loose from his hold and glared at Aileen. "I'll get you for this. Just see if I don't!"

Aileen stood outside and watched as the wagon pulled out of the yard. She walked inside to find Rosa sweeping up glass. "Here, let me do that." She tried to take the broom, but Rosa turned away out of Aileen's reach.

"No, *Señora*. This is my job, not yours." She thrust her chin toward the door. "Good riddance to Miss Ruth. She has been filling the *niño's* head with lies about her and Dr. Sam all the time he was gone."

Aileen could just imagine what she'd told the boy. Hopefully he'd confide in his father when they talked tonight. If so, Sam would tell her. To stay busy, she made beds and dusted. The guest room where Ruth had spent the night was in total disarray. Bed linens lay tossed on the floor. Why would she do such a thing—to make more work for Rosa?

She collected the sheets and pillowcases to wash and carried them into the kitchen. Rosa was stacking the clean dishes into a cabinet below a pie safe. "Where do you keep the dirty laundry until wash day?"

"Here, *Señora*. Let me take those." Before Aileen could protest, Rosa snatched them from Aileen's arms and led her to a large basket near the kitchen door. "I will do the laundry on Monday, unless *Señora* has need of something washed today."

"I thought I'd wash our clothes from the trip, but I can wait and do the task according to your schedule. I don't want to interfere with your routine."

Rosa slapped her hand against her heart. "The *señora* does not do laundry in this house. This is my chore. Scrubbing will ruin your beautiful hands."

"You might as well grow used to it, for I will not sit idle and let you do all of the work. This is my home now, and I want to take pride in how it is run and how it looks."

Rosa's expression of pleasure crumbled. "You are not satisfied with the *casa*? I will work harder."

"No, no, no, that's not it at all. I'm overjoyed at how well you manage the house. But I did not grow up to sit idle all day. I need to be working, to feel like I'm contributing to this family." Sure, she liked needlework and other womanly pursuits, but this was her home, and Sam and Tad were her family. She couldn't sit back and let someone else do everything for them. "Now, where are the clean linens kept? I'll get the bed in the guest room remade."

Aileen followed Rosa to a tall cabinet at the end of the hall that led to the bedrooms. Made of dark wood, with carving in intricate detail on each of the panels, it was polished to a high gloss. Aileen ran her hand along one of the panels—the surface as smooth as glass. "This is lovely."

"It was one of the first pieces of furniture Doctor Sam purchased after he finished his house." She unlocked the doors and lifted clean linens from the neat stack and handed them to Aileen. "In the drawers you will find towels and wash cloths."

"I've been meaning to ask, do we have a hip bath, or some type of tub?"

"Oh, yes. Behind the kitchen." Rosa showed Aileen the small room between the kitchen and the guest room. A large tub filled the end closest to the outside wall, where a tall window above it let in natural light. "The tub drain empties through a pipe that leads to the outside to water the garden. *Señora* Jane loved to work with the plants."

"What else did Jane like to do? Sam has told me very little about her."

Rosa laughed and shook her head. "She did not like kitchen work. Burned everything she tried to cook." Her gaze drifted to the kitchen. "She did like to show her china and put flowers in vases. Her needlework is all over the house." As if she'd said too much, she turned and left the room.

Aileen followed her. "What chores did she take over?"

"She was what Doctor Sam called delicate, so she did not do much. She washed their underclothes, dusted, and always set the table for me at dinner—made the beds, little touches here and there."

"What about Tad? Who kept an eye on him?"

"Ay-yi-yi, that *niño*." She laughed and shook her head. "*Señora* Jane tried to keep up with him, but as he got older, he wanted to spend his time outside in the barn and corral, so Miguel took to keeping a watch on him for her when Doctor Sam couldn't be here."

By lunchtime, Aileen had dusted the entire house, made the beds, and explored the area around the house. She decided to explore the barn. Tad, overjoyed with someone to talk to, tugged her into the hayloft to see the barn cat and her litter of seven kittens. "Aren't they cute, Aileen?"

"Yes, indeed, they are. We need a mouser for the house, don't you think?"

"Really?" His smile dropped. "Pa don't like cats inside. Said they're for the barn."

"Hmm. We'll talk to your da and try to change his mind." She shivered and gripped her arms. "Nothing gives the creeps more than mice and rats running around at night."

"Yea, and cats keep snakes away, too. That's why Rosa feeds them, so they'll hang around outside."

"Sounds like a good idea to me." She placed the kitten she'd been holding back beside its mother.

His face scrunched in concentration, he asked, "Which one do you like bestest, Aileen?"

She lifted the yellow kitten with black fur around her right eye. "This one, I think. She's nay pretty, but someday she'll be a loyal companion."

"How come? She might be mean."

"Have you noticed she's smaller than the other kittens and one of her legs doesn't work properly?" His gaze roamed the other six babies and then returned to the one she held.

"Yeah, so what?"

"I'm not an expert by any means, but I think the others and her mama push her aside. She has to fight for every drop of milk, so if she survives, she'll be a tough little mite."

His lip trembled. "Why would her ma treat her that way?" He sniffed, and Aileen feared he might tear up. She patted his shoulder. "Animal instincts are strong. The mama can tell when one is deformed and in many cases will not feed the weakest one. It's nature's way of keeping their blood line strong." She held this kitten close to her face and nuzzled its nose with hers. "But this little one will be fine. She's getting enough to eat, and when she's older, we'll see if we can come up with a way she can get around better."

His expression brightened. "Yeah, maybe Pa will fix her up."

Aileen chuckled. She had no idea how Sam would feel about treating animals. For his child, he wouldn't be able to say no. "He sure might. Come along now. Rosa will have lunch ready."

Chapter Thirteen

Grateful to spot home up ahead and ready for the feedbag, the mules hastened their pace. He knew exactly how they felt. Ruth's caterwauling all the way to town had been enough to put a stronger man in the ground. He'd let her rant, but when they arrived at her lodging, she'd climbed down before waiting for his help, and he'd been grateful to see her disappear inside.

Mary had come outside, her youngest baby on her hip, the other two hanging on to her skirt. "Morning, Sam. Could I interest you in a cup of coffee?"

"No, thanks, better see to my patients and head back home."

"Hear you brought home a wife, an Irish girl."

"Yes, I did. We'll stop by for a visit and make introductions one afternoon soon."

"I'd like that." She started back inside and then stopped. "It's good to have Ruth back with us. These kids are about to run me ragged."

He waved and prodded the mules into a slow plod. At Kruger's store, he checked the bulletin board for messages. Seemed no one needed him today.

Martha came out of the back room. "Morning, Sam. Need anything today?"

"Yes, I do. I overheard you whisper to Herman—for my benefit, I believe—that you have in your storeroom an entire batch of the dishes that match the tea set."

She chuckled. "Heard that, did ya?"

"Now, Martha, you know I did." He leaned against the counter. "Ruth broke one of the cups this morning, and I'd like to replace it."

"Ruth, huh? Bet she did it on purpose." She frowned. "Never liked the girl. She set her cap for you before Jane was cold in her grave. Wanted to give her a good smack."

Sam had had no idea the woman was so intent on catching his attention that soon. Oh, as time passed he'd noticed little things that caused suspicion to raise its ugly head, and some outward displays, but her behavior since he arrived home from Boston was an eye opener. "No worries, Martha. Aileen busted her lip this morning. Said Ruth broke the cup intentionally."

She slapped her knee in glee. "Knew that girl had spunk. Gave Ruth a little set-down, did she? Sure would like to have been there."

"It wasn't pretty. I don't know who lost more hair, Ruth or Aileen, but Aileen slammed her up against the wall." He couldn't help but grin. His wife wouldn't let anyone walk over her.

"Good for her. Maybe Ruth will stop putting on such airs around here. Thinks she's better than everybody else." Funny, Sam hadn't taken much notice until now. Had Jane been snooty also? No, she was sweet and likeable. But she hadn't been strong and resilient like Aileen. "Now, how many teacups would you be wantin'?"

Sam left Kruger's store with two crates of expensive china. The dinnerware cost almost as much as a good horse. What was he thinking? He stared at the gray hindquarters of his mules as they plodded along. Their tails swished back and forth to shoo away the flies. Ah, heck, he'd been thinking about the lone tear he'd seen on Aileen's face this morning. That's why he'd bought the china. He snorted. Who was he kidding? He'd planned to buy it anyway with the excuse she needed something of her own for the house.

He shook his head. No doubt about it. Aileen had wormed her way into his heart—something he did not want or need. That didn't mean he was in love with her. Loving someone and falling in love were two different emotions. Being in love meant taking a chance on getting hurt again, and he didn't need to experience that pain. Hurt? Who was he kidding?

****

Aileen woke to the sound of wagon wheels rolling across hard earth. *Sam is home.* She'd meant to rest her eyes a minute, but it appeared she'd slept for at least an hour. She rose and straightened the bed before splashing water on her face. Reaching for her tin of Lyon's Tooth Powder, she tapped out a small amount into her hand, added a little water, and using her boar bristle toothbrush, she scrubbed her teeth. She spit the rinse water into the chamber pot and rinsed her brush before putting it in the holder on the washstand.

As she neared the barn, she could hear Tad's excited voice talking to his pa. The occasional rumble of Sam's bass drifted to her between the boy's outbursts. "What's in that box, Pa?" Tad dogged Sam's heels as he lifted the crate and placed it on the ground.

"It's a surprise for Aileen." Her heart thumped with suspense. The box resembled the one that had held her tea set.

Tad climbed up on one of the spokes of a wagon wheel. He peered into the wagon bed. "Does 'Leen gots two surprises, Pa?" She smiled at Tad's abbreviation of her name.

"You'll find out soon enough." Sam carried another large container and positioned it on top of the other.

"Pa, what about my s'prise you was gonna bring from Boston?"

Sam yanked his hat off and slapped it against his leg. "By golly, you're right. We'll see about that as soon as I finish here and we get to the house."

Tad hopped down from the wheel spoke. "Here she comes, Pa." He ran toward her and grabbed her hand. "Come on, 'Leen. Pa's got two surprises for you."

Sam threw his hands up. "So much for surprises."

"You don't say?' She glanced at Sam. He grinned and winked. "I must have been a good girl, then."

Tad cocked his head and whispered, "I've been a good boy. Reckon Pa's got something for me?"

She leaned down and spoke softly. "I don't know. Guess we'll have to wait and see."

Sam joined them. With his arm around her shoulders, he placed a lingering kiss on her lips.

"Ewww, Pa...kissin' is disgusting." The scrunch of Tad's face reinforced his words.

"One of these days, you'll want to kiss a girl."

He shook his head. "Uh-uh, won't neither."

"We'll see." Sam lifted the boy and set him on his feet in the bed of the wagon. "If you look around in there, you might find another surprise."

Tad's eyes rounded. On hands and knees, he searched the area under the seat and then sat back on his heels. "All I sees, Pa, is this picnic basket." His shoulders sagged. "Shucks, I thought it might be a s'prise for me."

"Pull it out and take a look."

Miguel joined them at the wagon, and they all three propped their arms on the side to watch. Aileen didn't know for sure what was in the basket, but she had a good idea.

Tad sat with splayed legs and pulled the basket toward him. Movement under the napkin and a "yip, yip" had him squealing with glee. "A puppy, a puppy!" He yanked the cloth off to reveal a black-and-white splotched dog. It wasn't the most attractive dog she'd ever seen, but Tad was overjoyed. "Pa, you gots me one of Jessie's puppies!"

Tad squealed and laughed as the puppy crawled up his body and licked his face. "He likes me already, Pa."

"He sure does, son. He's your responsibility now."

"I know. I'll take good care of him."

"Hand him to me now, so you can climb down. We need to go up to the house so Aileen can open her surprise." Tad landed on his feet and reached for the puppy. "You think you can hold on to him?" Sam reached into the wagon to retrieve the basket and handed it to her. "Go ahead, if you will, and make sure Tad doesn't drop the animal on its head. I'll be along in a minute."

"You want me to carry him, Tad?"

"No, I gots him." He held the dog like a baby and nuzzled his fur. "He's so purty."

A lump formed in Aileen's throat. There was nothing more precious than a baby...of any species. "Do you have a name picked out?"

"Nope." He scrunched his mouth to one side. "I need to think on it some."

Sam and Miguel followed them to the house, each with a crate on his shoulder. Tad ran ahead, and she could hear Rosa making appreciative comments about their new family member. "Look at that black patch over his eye, *niño*. Why, you could call him Patches...or...how about Bandit?"

"That's it, that's it! The perfect name for him." He dashed into the dining room, where Aileen held the door to the patio open for the men. "Bandit! His name is Bandit, 'Leen." He rushed back to the kitchen. "Thank you, Rosa."

"You are welcome, Tad."

The men set the crates on the floor at the end of the sideboard. Miguel headed back out the door, and Sam squatted by the crate and, with a crow bar Miguel brought from the barn, pried up the lid of the first box. "Are you ready to see your surprise now, sweetheart, or do you prefer to wait?"

"I'm dying to see what's in there, though I have a good idea, but I think we should get Tad and his pup settled before I become too distracted."

He rose to his feet. "Good idea. Do you mind the pup being in the house?"

"Not at all." She looked at the boy. He was sitting with Bandit on the rug, and they played tug of war with a piece of rope she assumed he'd found in his pocket. "Though I do think until he's house trained he should stay off the rug."

"Good idea. I'll take them both outdoors and make sure Tad knows how to tell when he needs to take the pup outside."

"What breed of dog is he? I've never seen one like it before." In fact, he was downright ugly. Maybe he'd look better when grown.

"He's a cow dog. His breed works well with cattle and sheep and can withstand the arid temperature out here."

"Ah, that's good. He'll be a fine companion for Tad."

Aileen unpacked the dishes. With her finger, she traced the shamrock on the delicate porcelain. Loneliness stole over her, and for a moment, she had to swallow the tears that threatened. *Oh, Mam, I miss you so*. Her mother would have enjoyed helping her unpack and arrange the delicate set of Belleek, such an extravagance for use in this rough country. She wiped an errant tear off her cheek. What would Mam think about Sam?

Aileen glanced at the china adorning the shelves of the sideboard—Jane's set. Creamy white with delicate pink flowers, the china was almost as fragile as the shamrock-patterned ware. From the wedding picture hanging in the master bedroom, the china definitely reflected the woman's appearance—pale, with blonde hair. Aileen assumed her eyes were as blue as Tad's, and certainly she appeared fragile and easygoing.

Sam and Tad came into the house. "'Leen, Pa said whenever we see Bandit squat, we say 'no' and take him outside."

"Is that right?"

"Yeah, we don't want him doing his biz-nis in the house."

"Your pa is right, though every once in a while we may miss a signal and have to clean up after him."

He scrunched up his nose and tucked his chin. "Sure hope he don't. Cleanin' up poop and pee is disgusting." Aileen struggled to keep a straight face as he strode toward his bedroom. "Me and Bandit are gonna take a nap. Pa said pups need lots of sleep for growin'."

Sam hugged her to his side. "Thank you for being so accommodating about the dog."

"You're welcome." She turned, circled his waist with her arms, laid her head against his chest, and listened to the steady thump of his heart. "Thank you for the beautiful set of dishes."

He tilted her chin up to meet his descending mouth. "Anything to make my bride happy. And Ruth's behavior was despicable." His kiss sent any thought of Ruth skittering from her mind. She returned his kiss, their lips playful and savoring, eager to move closer. His tongue slipped inside her mouth and explored its recesses. Her knees weakened, and heat blossomed in her body. When he broke the embrace, she sagged in his arms, but he held her against him. He cleared his throat. "I'd better head back to the barn. Miguel will think I'm slacking." He wiggled his brows. "Or that I've taken you to bed for a nap."

Aileen slapped him on the chest. "Ach, get out of here, ya tease." Not to say she wouldn't be willing. Her face heated. He laughed and dropped a kiss to her forehead before striding out the door. Her heart sang from their playful banter. Sam could deny loving her all he wanted, but he did care, and enjoyed her company. It might not be love, but it was enough for now.

Aileen tiptoed into Tad's bedroom to check on the boy. He lay sound asleep, the puppy cuddled against his side. Sweat-dampened hair clung to his face. Bandit lifted his head, thumped his tail, and yawned before burying his nose against Tad again. She stepped to the window and opened one of the sashes to allow airflow between the bedroom and the open doors in the living area. Satisfied he was comfortable, she set to unpacking her china.

****

"Pa, Pa, Bandit piddled on the floor." Sam tossed hay into the mules' stall and turned to the boy. He carried the pup in his arms, but made to set him down.

"Whoa, whoa, now. We can't turn him loose in the barn until he learns these animals could step on him. Plus, his barking would scare them. Especially the chickens—why, they might quit laying."

Tad looked over to the chicken coop. "You're teasing about the chickens, right, Pa?"

"No, son, I'm not." Sam had fashioned a leash for the pup out of some old worn-out reins. He'd cut out the good pieces and tied them together to form a length of rawhide that would suit. He tied one end around Bandit's neck and handed the other one to Tad. "Don't let him loose in here. Matter of fact, until he learns the rules, he has to stay tied unless he's in the house."

"Aw, that's terrible, Pa."

"It's better than him running off and a coyote or wolf having him for dinner. Wouldn't you agree?"

Tad's eyes rounded, and he nodded. "Yes, sir, Pa. I'll keep him close."

Sam tousled the blond head. "Now, what's this about piddling?"

"'Leen calls peeing piddling." A giggle lit his face. "Ain't that funny?"

"Now you have a new word to use."

"'Spect so."

"Was Aileen mad? Did she scold you?"

"Nah. She told Bandit 'no, no' and took him out to the patio. He explored for a while and found a patch of grass and piddled some more. She picked him up and rubbed his belly and told him what a good boy he was."

Pleased with his wife's actions, he asked, "What about the mess in the house?"

"She gots one of your old work shirts from the dirty clothes and wet one end of it from the sink. Then she wiped up the pee with the dry end and then washed over it with the wet end."

Well, Sam was pleased she'd at least chosen a work shirt.

Tad cocked his head. "Did you know we had to get the pee odor up or he'll pee there again?"

"Yes, son, I did, and I'm glad Aileen knew too."

"She's smart, ain't she, Pa?"

"Indeed she is, son." Sam hid his smile. Maybe the boy would take to Aileen faster than he'd hoped. Tad still remembered his mother, and it was only natural for him to be loyal to her memory. "Now, you take Bandit for a walk before dinner. Give him time to smell things along the way. Dogs have a powerful sense of smell, and that's how he'll learn about his new home." That ought to keep him occupied until time for dinner. He chuckled at Tad's dialogue as he walked.

"No, no, Bandit. That there is cow poop. Shoo-wee, it stinks. Don't be gettin' it on your feet, or Rosa won't let you in the house."

An hour later the boy and his dog returned. "I showed him all around the house, Pa. He piddled on almost every plant we passed…even on the pump."

"That's his way of marking his territory so other animals will know this is his space."

Tad looked around their yard, deep in thought. "Wow, Pa. You sure are smart."

"You will be too one day, son." He clapped him on the shoulder. "Let's head for the house. I bet supper is ready."

Aileen had prepared a mixture of milk and leftover biscuits for the puppy. She'd set two bowls on the floor in the kitchen by the back door—one for his food, and the other for water. He gobbled it down and immediately squatted to pee. "No, Bandit."

He reached for the pup, but Aileen beat him to it. She lifted the dog and headed out the back door. "You two get washed up for supper. We'll be right back."

Tucked into his basket afterward, Bandit went right to sleep. Sam knew it would be necessary to spend some time with Tad to make sure he was aware how dropping the puppy could hurt him. Sam had been pleased when the boy mentioned Aileen's preference for the kitten with the damaged leg. They'd fashioned a brace with twigs and old rags. In a week or so they'd bring the kitten into the house.

Sam held Aileen's chair as she sat down. She smiled up at him. "Thank you, Sam."

After the blessing, Tad talked nonstop. Sam wasn't sure how the boy got any food eaten, but his plate was almost cleaned.

"Slow down, Tad. It's bad manners to hog the conversation at the table."

He lowered his head. "Sorry, Pa."

"It's okay because I know you're excited." He

looked over to the sideboard and Aileen's new china displayed neatly. "Your new dishes look nice in here."

"They do, don't they?"

Tad looked up from his plate and stared at the new pieces. Gone was the face of the excited boy. His face scrunched up as tears pooled in his eyes. He glared at Aileen. "Where's my ma's dishes?" He shoved his plate back, and Sam grabbed his glass of milk before it turned over. "I hate you! You're not my mother…and…her plates was purtier than your ugly old stuff."

Chapter Fourteen

Sam, a frown covering his face, stared at her. "Where are Jane's things?"

"They're packed in the boxes my china came in."

"You could have given the boy some time to grow used to you before removing his mother's things." He shoved his chair back and stood.

"I'm sorry, Sam. I had no idea he'd be so upset over the change."

"Well, get things changed back tomorrow. Give him more time." He turned and strode toward Tad's room.

"I'll do no such thing." She'd risen without realizing it. "I kept a few of Jane's pieces out for Tad to decide where to display them. The remainder is packed for him to give to his wife when he marries."

Regret crossed his face, and he stretched a hand out to her. "Aileen...forgive me—"

"Don't bother with apologies. See to your son." Holding her hurt inside, she started clearing the table. If Sam wasn't finished eating, well, that was just too darn bad. She scraped the contents of Tad's plate onto Sam's and carried them to the kitchen. Bandit's bowl sat empty by the back door, so she crumbled the leftover bread into his bowl. Rosa had washed her preparation dishes before she left for home, so Aileen quickly washed what they'd used for their meal and put them away.

Just as she left the kitchen, Tad ran to her and threw his arms around her waist. Face pressed against her, he sobbed, "I'm...sorry, sorry...'Leen. Pa 'splained to me."

She dropped to her knees and hugged him close. "Now, now, 'tis okay. I should have waited to explain me plans before I got carried away putting the dishes out. But I'm so proud of what your pa bought for me, I couldn't wait to display them." She wiped his eyes with the hem of her skirt and then stood and took his hand. "Let's look at what I thought you might like to display of your mother's. It's for you to decide."

They stopped before the sideboard. Against the dark, heavy wood, her dishes stood out to advantage, just as Jane's had. Aileen lifted his mother's gravy boat for Tad's inspection. "This would look fine in front of your ma's large serving platter. And since they'll be handy, we can use them from time to time, if you'd like." She lined the plate up in the rail on the lowest shelf and placed the other item in front. "Now, how does that look to you?"

His gaze flitted between her china pieces along with those of his mother's. "Purty." He pointed. "Look, Ma's dishes have some of the same green leaves as yours."

"Yes, they do." She led him to the corner the packing crates occupied. "These are the rest of your mother's dishes, safely packed away for when you marry."

"Aw, I don't think I'll get married. Don't like girls much."

"Well, we'll keep them stored for you in the barn,

in case you change your mind."

"Okay."

Sam laid a hand on Tad's shoulder. "Best give Bandit a chance at his dishes again, and then take him out, so he will be ready to settle for the night."

Tad scampered off, tears forgotten. Sam caught her shoulders and slid his hand across to cup her face. "I am sorry for jumping to conclusions." He dropped his forehead to hers. "I should have known you'd not intentionally upset Tad."

She clasped his shirtfront. "Please remember that fact the next time." Stepping out of his grasp, she walked toward the bedroom. With the washstand ewer in her hand, she proceeded to the kitchen to draw hot water.

Sam took the pitcher. "Here, let me take that for you."

"Thank you. I'll get the one from Tad's room so you can give him a good wash. I don't think he's ready for me to take on that chore just yet."

Tad and Bandit rushed in from the back door. "He did just like you said, Pa. He sniffed every little thing and piddled on them all, and then pooped." He wrinkled his nose. "It sure do stink."

Sam ruffled his hair. "That's why we want him to do his business outside. Did you remember to praise him when he finished?"

"Sure did. He's one smart dog. I think he'll be trained right quick."

"We'll see. Now put him in his basket, and let's get you washed and ready for bed."

****

The days slipped into weeks and then into a month.

Aileen settled into a routine of sorts. Sam had brought in the lame cat. He'd fashioned a brace to help straighten its leg. Tad had named her Patches because of the patch over her eye, and she and Bandit kept them laughing with their scampering play about the house.

A letter arrived from Lydia. She'd been hired at a milliner's shop and loved making a variety of hats. Even though she could afford a small place, Uncle Avery insisted she live at home until she married, not that she had a beau just yet.

Sam made love to Aileen often, but he never uttered the words she so wanted to hear. She'd not conceived, and the fear she might be barren haunted her. Though she was happy in her new life, a babe would make her ecstatic.

Sam and Miguel worked with the livestock. Tad and Bandit trailed along behind them during the mornings. The pup was quickly learning to stay out of the way of the animals and might soon be of help. The afternoons were spent at the house, with Bandit learning commands—fetch, sit, and stay. The heat was too much for Tad to stay out for long after noon. He'd grow accustomed to the temperature as summer progressed, Sam told Aileen. *I wonder how long it will take me?* It was scorching, and she stayed in the shade under the grape arbor as much as possible when outdoors. In the early mornings, she worked in the vegetable garden.

Early evenings, after Tad had washed and readied for bed, they played Parcheesi, Sam's surprise from Boston for his son. She and Sam were evenly matched, and Tad's skill improved every day. Some nights they read stories. Sam had a shelf full of books, so they never lacked for material.

One morning, after visiting patients, Sam came home with a pretty chestnut horse trailing the wagon. Aileen saw the cart as it passed the house. She dried her hands on a dishtowel and ran out to the barn. Sam led the animal up to her. "What do you think about her?"

Tad jumped up and down. "Ain't she purty, 'Leen?"

She ran her hands down the mare's sleek neck and back. "Yes, she is, Tad." She tweaked his nose. "And it's, 'Isn't she pretty?' We need to work on your grammar." He'd be going to school in the fall, but it didn't hurt to get a head start.

He scrunched up one side of his face. "That's what I said."

Aileen threw up her hands. She frowned at Sam. "You could help me out here."

He coughed into his hand. "Now, Tad, 'ain't' is not a proper word. You need to try to remember to say 'isn't.'"

"Why?"

"Because you'll be going to school in September, and you'll want to be able to speak correctly."

"Okay, Pa. I'll try."

Satisfied that Tad had registered what his father said, she returned her attention to the mare. "She's beautiful, Sam. Who's going to ride her?"

"Why, you are, sweetheart. She's yours."

His wide, proud smile melted her heart. At a loss for words, she threw her arms around his neck and squeezed. "I love you, Sam. Thank you."

He froze for a moment and then hugged her close. "You're welcome." He pulled back. "Run put on your riding skirt, and we'll take a ride."

She did as he requested, and when mounted, she asked, "What's her name?"

"She's been called June Bug, but we can change it if you want."

"Oh, no. It fits her perfectly. Though I'm sure I'll enjoy her a lot more than I do those pesky critters that flit around."

Aileen was in heaven. The desert floor lay spread out before them, and they galloped across the terrain. "Most of the land in this creek bed is free of rabbit holes, so it's safe for a full gallop. During rainy weather, it can become a death pit, though, as flash floods come through in a hurry."

They climbed out of the gulley and started back home. "Along here you may find rabbit burrows your horse might step in and a variety of cactus you want to avoid while riding."

She saw what looked somewhat like a rabbit scurrying out of their way. "If that's a rabbit, it must be deformed. Look at its ears. They're huge."

"It's a jackrabbit. Those big ears help keep it cool in this desert heat."

"Really?"

"Would I lie to you?"

"No, but you might tease me a bit."

He moved his horse closer to hers. With his hand behind her head, he pulled her nearer and leaned over to plant a kiss on her lips. "I promise to always tell you the truth about things that matter."

****

A few months later, when Bandit was six months old, Sam sat down on the sofa with Tad for a chat.

Aileen finished removing the supper dishes while they talked. She wasn't sure how Sam's news would go over with the boy.

"Bandit is growing bigger and smarter every day, isn't he?"

"He sure is, Pa. I reckon we can take his leash off afore too long."

"Hmm, I'm not sure, son."

"Why not? Don't you think he's smart enough?"

"Of course he is, but…he's not been trained to be a cow dog."

Tad jumped up off the sofa. "I can train him, Pa. I've taught him to sit and stay. He even comes when I call him."

Aileen joined them and picked up her mending. Tad's britches grew new holes every day.

"I expect you could, son, but the best teacher for him is his mother."

Tad cocked his head. "But Jessie don't live here."

"That's right." Sam pulled Tad between his legs and held his arms. "So Bandit can become the best cow or sheep dog he can be, he needs to be trained by Jessie and her owner. He'll just be gone a month, maybe a little longer."

Tad's bottom lip drooped, and he crossed his arms. "Can we go visit him?"

"No, because we'll distract him from his lessons." Tears gathered in the boy's eyes, and Aileen held her breath as she waited for a tantrum. It didn't happen.

"Well, I don't like it none, but I 'spect we have to do what's best for him." He raised his eyes to his father's. "We sure don't want him to be a bad cow dog, do we?"

Sam pulled him close and patted his back. "You're absolutely right. And, because you've been so grown up about this, after we leave Bandit, we'll come home and play the game we brought from Boston."

****

Tad, holding Bandit in his lap, talked the entire trip to the ranch where Jessie lived. An expression of humor on his face, Sam chuckled and said, "Reckon we can leave Tad with Bandit for some training?"

"Oh, Pa, you's so silly. I'm already trained up just fine." He peered up at Aileen. "Ain't I, 'Leen?"

"Aren't you, Tad." She put her arm around his shoulders and hugged the boy to her side. "Your pa was teasing. Humans can't learn everything they need to know about cows and sheep as fast as dogs can." At least that's what she thought. "You'll learn from your pa and Miguel."

Sam patted Tad's leg. "I'm proud of how you're handling this, son."

He buried his face in Bandit's coat. He mumbled, "You learn fast, boy, so you can come home, ya hear?"

Bandit yipped, and they all laughed.

Leaving the pup upset Tad more than expected after his brave front. Sam pulled the wagon to a stop, put on the brake, and lifted his son to his lap. "It's all right to cry. Seems our heart doesn't ache as much when we do."

His sobs broke Aileen's heart. When he pulled back from Sam and wiped the moisture from his face, she patted his back. "Feel better now?"

He sniffed and wiped his nose on his sleeve. "Some, but I'm shore gonna miss him."

"I think we all will. He's a cute little bugger.

Though he's not going to be little much longer." The dog was already an armful for Tad to carry. "Patches will miss him too, so you need to give her a little extra attention."

Sam released the brake and set the mules in motion again. "Let's stop by Kruger's store before heading home. Be thinking about what we need."

"We need flour, I know, and if we can't find Tad a couple pair of pants, I need fabric to make him some." She ruffled his hair. "His pants are getting so holey, I'm running out of places to sew on patches."

He giggled. "Aw, Mam, you're so funny." His big blue eyes studied her face.

Her heart thrummed and pressure pulsed in her ears. Fearing the organ would jump out of her chest, she used her hand to keep it in place. "Did...did you call me...Mam?"

"Uh-huh." His bottom lip trembled, and he used his teeth to still it. "Are you mad?"

She hugged him close and kissed the top of his head. "I'm delighted."

"Then how come you gots watery eyes?"

"'Cause I'm happy."

Chapter Fifteen

"Let's go, Tad." The boy played in the dirt, drawing different designs. "Time to leave for town." Tonight was the community's Saturday night social. The adults were already in the wagon waiting for him. He dropped the stick and came running.

"Comin', Pa." Miguel picked him up and set him in the wagon bed on quilts Aileen had packed in case the boy grew sleepy before the festivities were over.

As soon as Tad settled, Sam flicked the reins. "Go, boys." Delicious odors wafted up from the back. Sam had sampled a spoonful of the beans so could attest to their flavor. He intended to join the food line early on so he wouldn't face an empty dish.

Rosa and Aileen had spent all day baking pies, preparing Boston baked beans, and frying chicken to add to the food table. During years past, the tabletop had gotten so heavy they had to shove extra sawhorses under the pieces of lumber to keep the loaded slab from collapsing.

As soon as they arrived at the courthouse, men came forward to help them unload. Aileen and Rosa followed along and supervised the placement of their dishes, while Sam and Miguel moved the wagon. They unhitched the mules and walked them over to the springs so they could graze and enjoy the fresh water.

The band, which included a harp picker and a

violin player, had a makeshift stage at one end of the room. As they warmed up, a crowd formed, waiting for the dancing to begin. Sam watched as Aileen visited with Suzy Smithson. The two had become good friends and visited back and forth. Aileen's tea set enjoyed a lot of use.

Someone clapped him on the back. "Hey, Sam." It was Tom Smithson.

"How are you, Tom?"

"I'm good but beginning to worry about Suzy. Her morning sickness is so bad she's flat on her back all morning."

Poor woman. Sam felt for her. He'd been told the dry heaves in the mornings was the worst sick there could be. "Have her drink ginger tea in the mornings." He clasped Tom's shoulder in sympathy. "Give her a few more weeks. She should feel better by then."

Their wives joined them. Snuggled against her husband's side, Suzy appeared the picture of health, so Sam was content with the advice he'd given Tom.

Aileen tucked her arm under his. "I think it's time you proved to me you can dance."

"Well, hang on to your hat, then." He twirled her around the floor to a waltz, leaving her breathless when they stopped. "Did I do okay, sweetheart?"

Her cheeks were flushed, and her eyes glittered in the glow of kerosene lamps suspended from the ceiling, while the red dress she wore enhanced the red in her dark, auburn hair. "I'd say you did more than okay."

He'd never seen her more beautiful. Her smile of joy melted his heart. He pulled her into a tight embrace, and his lips slanted across hers and drank their fill.

Embarrassed, Aileen pushed against his chest.

"Sam…stop it. We have an audience."

He pulled her face to his shoulder as the band started a slow number. "I don't care. A man should be able to kiss his wife anytime he wants."

She nodded toward the group of kids openly staring. "Even in front of your son and his friends?"

"Guess you got me there." His son in particular appeared very interested. "All this exercise has made me hungry. You ready to grab a plate and find a place to sit down and eat?"

"Yes, I'm hungry also. Let's go get Tad."

Just as they sat down outside on one of Aileen's quilts, Miguel and Rosa joined them. "Is there enough room for two more?"

Several hours later, they loaded the wagon and headed for home. Some families who lived farther away had come prepared to spend the night so they could attend church on Sunday. A guest pastor would be giving the sermon, and he was a favorite with the community. Though the church was Catholic, the sanctuary was made available to other denominations.

"Pa, I sure wish we could spend the night. I ain't never gotten to sleep in a tent."

"Haven't ever, son." Tad groaned. Sam chuckled. "Some weekend we'll see about pitching a tent."

"Really, Pa? Oh, boy, can Bandit come too?"

"Of course."

Satisfied, he quieted. Sam suspected Tad would be asleep in no time at all.

When Sam pulled the wagon into the barn, Miguel hopped off the back end. "Go ahead and take the *niño* to bed. I'll take care of the mules."

"Are you sure, Miguel?

"*Si.*"

Aileen began to load dishes into a small crate.

"Just leave them for tonight," Sam told her. "We'll retrieve them in the morning." They were all empty, so no need to worry about food disappearing. Of course, they'd probably be covered in ants. He lifted Tad into his arms and carried him into the house, where Aileen hurried to turn back the covers on Tad's bed. Sam laid him on the sheet and stripped his shoes and pants. "That ought to do for tonight."

She brushed the hair out of the boy's face. "I'd love to give him a light wash, but it would probably wake him." She leaned down and laid a kiss on his forehead.

Sam bent over and kissed his cheek. "Night, buddy."

"Night, Pa." He turned onto his side, nuzzled his head on the pillow a second, and stilled.

They walked across the hall to their bedroom. Sam lit the lamp on the vanity and turned the wick up enough to cast a soft glow. "While I draw us some warm water, you go ahead and brush your hair. Leave it loose tonight."

She cocked her head and grinned. "Are you going to help me untangle it in the morning?"

"Yes, ma'am."

She turned her back to him. "Unbutton me first, will you?"

He loosened the dress and pressed a kiss between her shoulder blades. She shivered.

When he returned, she sat at the vanity in her shift, brushing her hair. Under the dim light, her beautiful skin and hair glowed. He was a lucky man. He cleared his throat. "Here we are. You go first."

While she washed, he slipped out of his clothes. She slipped her gown over her head and lifted the bowl to toss the water outside. "Here, let me." He made quick work of tossing it on the grapevine just outside the door. By the time he finished washing, Aileen was in bed, almost asleep.

He slid beneath the sheet and pulled her into his arms. Her hair fanned out across his arm, and he ran his fingers through the soft strands. "Did you have fun tonight?"

"Oh, yes, a wonderful time." She ruffled the hairs on his chest. "And you, my husband, are a fine dancer." Arms across his chest, she nuzzled his neck. "Sam...do you think I'm barren?"

"What brought this to mind?"

"Suzy and Tom are expecting a baby. And I don't know for sure, but I think Rosa might be pregnant." A tear dropped onto his chest.

"Oh, sweetheart. We'll have a babe one day." He stroked her back, hoping the action would sooth her tears and his guilt. He'd been so selfish, but she'd known his thoughts on the matter from the beginning. Who knew his remorse would eat away at him?

"But...but...you don't want more children. You've told me so several times."

"I know. I suppose I'm a coward. Many women die during childbirth." And numerous newborns died before having a chance at life.

"I'm strong, Sam." She pulled his hands to her hipbone. "My hips are wide enough for carrying and delivering a child." She sniffed and slapped him on the belly. "Please stop using those French letters. I want to bear a child…our child, Sam."

"All right, my love." They'd not discussed the condoms. He was surprised that, with her outspoken ways, she was just now voicing her opinion. "Let's see if we can make it happen."

She drew him close and placed soft, gentle kisses across his chest, and then up to seal her lips to his. He rolled her to her back and deepened the kiss. And for the first time since their marriage, he didn't reach for the box of condoms behind his Bible in the drawer of his bedside table.

****

Aileen rose early to stoke the fire and help Rosa in the kitchen. Folks who lived in town or close enough to travel back and forth in a short period of time prepared food for a get-together after services. Thank goodness they wouldn't be plucking chickens. She'd brought in a large smoked ham yesterday for Sunday lunch. Just as she slid it in one side of the oven, Rosa opened the back door.

"Morning, *Señora*."

"Good morning, Rosa."

Rosa hesitated and then rushed back outside. Aileen hurried out to ask if she could help and found the woman retching. She rubbed her back in soothing circles. "Come along now. Have a lie-down on the couch, and I'll fetch a cool washcloth." Fortunately they had water pumped into the house. She wet a washcloth and handed it to Rosa.

"Thank you." Rosa wiped her mouth and face and then laid the cloth across her neck. "I'm sorry to trouble you."

"You are no trouble." She grabbed a pillow from

the end of the sofa and stuffed it behind Rosa's head. "Now, just close your eyes. I'll brew you a cup of ginger tea." She glanced back at the young woman. "It's the morning sickness, isn't it?" Rosa's big smile was the only answer Aileen needed. "I'm so happy for you."

An hour later, Rosa was up and preparing breakfast. Sam opened the back door and came inside. "Miguel and Rosa are joining us for breakfast, sweetheart." He grinned and winked at Rosa. "Seems we had a bout of nausea this morning." She ducked her head in embarrassment. He put an arm around Rosa's shoulders. "Hey, congratulations. It's going to be a beautiful baby if he takes after you."

"Who's having a baby?"

Tad walked in barefooted and barelegged. He gazed at both Aileen and Rosa.

Sam scooped him up. "Let's get you dressed first, and we'll share the news at breakfast."

****

Church services were well attended. Some of the people hadn't been at the dance the evening before. Sam knew almost everyone and introduced her to those she hadn't met yet. She still had a difficult time remembering all the names, but the more often she saw them, the easier it became. Tad saw Ruth and ran to her. The woman hugged the boy and then took his hand.

"Come say hi to Pa and Mam."

"And who?"

"Mam. I call her Mam."

Ruth caught his shoulders and shook. "That woman is not your mother. You hear me?"

Aileen was near enough to hear the exchange and

reached them just as Tad broke away from Ruth and ran to Aileen. His arms clutched her waist.

"I think the entire congregation heard you, Ruth," Aileen told her. Sure enough, heads were together, and talk buzzed among the crowd. "If you can't accept the way things are, I suggest you stay away from Tad unless he's with Sam or me."

She felt Sam's hand on her shoulder and glanced up to observe the anger in his eyes. "You'd best heed what Aileen says, Ruth."

Ruth turned on her heel and stalked out of the sanctuary.

Tad, chin trembling, pulled on Sam's pant leg. "Pa, why don't Aunt Ruth want me to call 'Leen Mam?"

Sam leaned down so they were face to face. "I guess she's afraid you'll forget your ma, and she may resent Aileen for trying to take that place." Aileen wanted to issue a loud snort. The woman was jealous and wanted to be Sam's wife. He tapped Tad on the nose. "Don't you be worrying about it now. Let's enjoy church, and we'll discuss this more later, if you want."

With one hand at her waist and the other on Tad's shoulder, Sam escorted them to a pew close to the front. Tad sat between her and Sam, nodding and then jerking his head back up. Finally she put her arm around his shoulders. He nestled into her side and soon slept.

Later, as they approached the wagon, a very much awake Tad hollered, "Bandit, Bandit!"

Chapter Sixteen

Sam spent the night at the Payton ranch delivering a baby boy. The father passed out and hit his head on the fireplace. The wound required twelve stitches. Thank goodness Mrs. Payton's mother was there to help out. On his way home, he passed through town and stopped at the general store to see Herman and Martha and check the bulletin board.

"Howdy, Sam. You look tuckered out."

"That I am."

Herman slipped a bottle of prime brandy out from under the counter. "How about a little snort?"

"Don't mind if I do." He tossed the heady brew down. The warmth hit his stomach and spread. The heat felt mighty good.

"Want another?"

He turned his glass over. "No, one's my limit on an empty stomach. I hope the Paytons' baby boy was my only patient for the day." He went to the bulletin board to check if he had any messages and blew out a sigh of relief to find it empty.

"You know Martha would be pleased to fix you some grub. She's right fond of you, you know."

"Much obliged, but Aileen will be worried if I don't get home soon." Last night's birth had taken longer than usual.

"How'd she like those purty dishes you bought

her?"" Herman leaned across the counter and whispered, "You know Martha put that bug in your ear a purpose, don't ya?"

Sam chuckled. "Your wife didn't have me fooled one bit. I'm grateful to her, though. The set was the perfect gift for Aileen." He glanced around the store. He should've asked before he left home if they needed anything. Nothing came to mind. "Goodbye, Herman. Tell Martha hello for me."

"I'll do it."

****

Quinton Lynch had never been more uncomfortable in his life. If he'd known what stagecoach travel would be like when they'd sailed for Boston, he'd have jumped overboard. It had been a horrible trip. The train wouldn't have been so bad if not for sharing a berth with Brian, but the man wore that noxious sweet toilet water and hogged the covers. It'd been durned cold from Boston to Oklahoma. He pulled at his collar. Now, he was sweltering.

Lynch glared at MacAuley. He shared a seat with two ladies—mother and daughter. Naturally the daughter was in the middle, and Brian did his best to ogle every inch of the young woman's bosom he could, even moved his arm so it would graze her breast. She shied away from him. Her mother snored blissfully. He shook his head in disgust. The cowboys next to Quinton didn't smell too good, but at least the body odor was from hard work. From the glares they sent Brian, they'd had about enough of the man's disrespect.

One of the men stood and yelled out the window at the driver. "Stop the coach."

A few minutes later, the driver yanked the door

open. "What's the problem in here, Jake?"

"This Mr. MacAuley has been making free"—he nodded at the young woman—"with the young lady's person."

Brian drew himself up and puffed out his chest. "I beg your pardon. I did no such thing."

The driver's glance scanned each person and stopped on the lady. "Miss?"

Her face reddened, but she nodded.

Like a shot, the driver's meaty fist grabbed Brian's coat front and yanked him from the coach. MacAuley stumbled and fell on his bum in the dirt.

"You can't do this to me! I paid my fare just like everyone else."

"Mister, I only state the rules once. You don't follow them, you walk." He mounted the stage and threw Brian's suitcase and a canteen of water down. "Follow this road and you should reach Fort Stockton in about six hours." They heard the crack of the driver's whip, and the coach jerked forward.

One of the cowboys threw MacAuley's hat out the window and yelled, "Watch out for rattlesnakes. It's that time of year."

Quinton took out his watch. The time read four in the afternoon. Brian wouldn't make it to town until around ten...if he survived that long. He struggled to keep from laughing. The pompous baboon—he deserved to be made a laughing stock. These Texans didn't put up with any misbehavior on the vehicle. Probably didn't anywhere, when it came to their women.

When they unloaded in Fort Stockton, Quinton wandered into the saloon next to the mercantile to wait for Brian. A few patrons eyed him warily as he made his way to the bar.

"I'll have a beer, if ya please."

The bartender poured him a mug and named his price. Quinton laid a few coins on the counter. "Where you from, mister?"

Quinton eyed the brew. It looked as weak as every other beer he'd had in the States. He took a swig and tried not to let his distaste show. "Cork County, Ireland."

"You don't say." He chuckled. "Could tell you was from some foreign country." He stuck his hand out. "Dewitt Jones. Folks here call me Witt."

Quinton shook the proffered hand and shook. "Quinton Lynch."

"What brings you to Fort Stockton?"

"Personal business I'm not at liberty to discuss."

Witt arched a bushy brow. "The law after you? If so, march right out uh here. We don't harbor criminals."

Quinton stiffened his back. "I'll have you know I'm a law-abiding citizen."

Witt lowered his brow and nodded. "Good to hear." He threw the dishtowel he'd been wiping glasses with over his shoulder. "You hungry? Still got a little chili left in the pot. Corn bread, too."

Quinton's stomach rumbled in anticipation.

The bartender's large belly bounced up and down as he chuckled. "Guess that's a yes." He waved to a table, and Quinton carried his mug over and sat down. He was close to the game of cards going on.

"Hey, mister. Join us for a game of cards?"

Quinton turned so he could assess the men. They

were wiley and rough; he wouldn't fare well in their company, plus he couldn't afford to lose any more money. "I appreciate the offer, gentlemen, but I must decline. Maybe another time."

He turned back to find a bowl of meat in front of him. Dark red in color, it didn't resemble anything he'd been served before but smelled delicious. The butter on the cornbread melted and slid down onto the plate. His mouth watered as he reached for a slice.

"Where you stayin'?"

"I don't know. Can you recommend a place where I can rent a room?"

He folded his hands over the apron covering his large belly. "You can spread your bedroll on the floor of the saloon for a dollar."

"Don't have a bedroll." He took a swallow of beer. "You don't have a boarding house?"

"We got one, but it's run by Mrs. Arbuckle…hee-hee…no relation to the coffee, but she's only got one room, and she's mighty picky 'bout who she rents to. Finish your eats, and I'll tell you how to get to her house."

"Thank you." The man watched as Quinton bit into the cornbread and nodded his head in appreciation. With a grin on his face, he waited while Quinton scooped a spoonful of the chili into his mouth. Quinton chewed and swallowed. "It's good. A little spicy, but I'll manage." He lifted his mug. "I'll have another."

"Coming right up."

Comments and sniggers drifted over from the card game: "Bet he don't make it halfway through the bowl," and, "He sure talks funny. Just like that pretty little wife of Doc's."

At the last comment, Quinton's spoon halted halfway to his mouth. He swallowed, the tension churning in his gut, and continued to eat the spicy dish…it grew hotter with each mouthful. He followed each spoonful with a chunk of cornbread. Heat rose in his face, and he drank his beverage down to cool his palate. His nose ran and his eyes watered. He withdrew his handkerchief to wipe his eyes and nose.

Every eye in the room was on him, waiting for his reaction. He'd finish the chili or burn to a cinder trying. When he'd scraped the bowl clean and downed his third beer, he leaned back in his chair and issued a loud belch. His mouth and belly burned like the devil danced a jig inside his innards. He sighed with relief and leaned back in the chair to finish his brew.

Witt walked outside with him and directed him to Mrs. Arbuckle's boarding house down the street. As luck would have it, her only room was available. The wizened little lady gave strict orders. "You'll take a full bath in the spring before sleeping on my bed linens." She handed him two towels and a bar of awful-smelling soap.

Quinton returned to the bar to wait for Brian. Just before midnight, he stumbled into the saloon with an obvious limp. He dropped his bag just inside the door and yelled, "Water."

"Here you go, mister." Witt set a glass on the bar. Brian guzzled it down and shoved the glass forward for a refill. Dirt covered his face and clothes. Some of what looked like dirt was really sunburn. The man would be in pain for a few days.

"Got kicked off the stage, did ya?"

"Yes, and I'm going to report that driver to the

sheriff and the stage line." He turned and located Quinton. "And you. You could've taken up for me."

Quinton swallowed his laugh. "Too many witnesses against you."

Brian snorted. "You could have gotten out and walked in with me."

"Why? You wouldn't have if I'd been kicked off."

The table of men was all ears now. The oldest of the gentlemen asked, "Why'd you get thrown off?"

Another added, "Did it have something to do with the purty little lady that stepped off the stage with her mama? 'Cause if it does, you'd best make yourself scarce. Her fee-on-say is a captain at Fort Davis. If he finds out, he'll teach you a lesson or two."

"I'm tired of being accused of something I didn't do."

Witt snorted. "Why'd they'd toss you off, then?"

"The whole bunch of passengers had it in for me, that's why."

Witt spit, barely missing the toe of Brian's boot.

He jumped back and glared at the man.

"That'll be four bits for the water."

"What? That's highway robbery." He waved his hand at the open door. "You got a whole spring full out there."

"Got that right, mister. Give me my money, and get out there and start lapping."

****

Quinton had long appreciated Aileen's refusal to marry Brian. The man was a bully and complained more than a woman. His yell when he hit the cold water of Comanche Springs was enough to draw the entire town. Thank goodness it didn't. No doubt it was cold, but Quinton didn't want an audience.

The soap stank, but it did the job. In short time, he'd scrubbed his body and clothes, and stood on the bank drying off with Mrs. Arbuckle's towel. He withdrew clean clothes from his bag and dressed. At least they'd had sense enough to purchase extras in Odessa.

"Hurry up, Brian. If we're too late, Mrs. Arbuckle may not let us in."

"She already has our money, doesn't she?"

"Yes, but the lady isn't the sweet sort. Looks like she'd shoot you if you blinked wrong."

"Oh, all right." He quickly dried and dressed. In just their socks, they carried their bags, shoes inside, across the road and down the street, limping and cursing as rocks and other debris bruised their tender soles.

Mrs. Arbuckle had left a coal oil lamp lit so they could find their way to their room. They fell into bed, and Brian's loud snore shook the bed almost as soon as his head touched the pillow. Quinton's last thought before succumbing to slumber was that he'd not tell Brian that Aileen had been mentioned in the saloon.

Chapter Seventeen

"Breakfast is ready, gentlemen." Evidently Brian's sweet talk and fancy manners had won Mrs. Arbuckle over. Of course that added another dollar to her pocket. Quinton wouldn't complain. After his introduction to chili the evening before, his time in the outhouse this morning had been quite painful. He hoped eggs and biscuits would calm his digestive tract.

An hour later, they were at Johnson's Livery, where Brian negotiated with the man on the rental of two horses. They agreed on a price, and the man led out two mares, both beautiful animals but nothing like the ones Quinton had owned in Ireland. "You fellas from Ireland?"

"Yes, indeed," quipped Brian. "Anyone else in Fort Stockton from Ireland?"

"Not that I've met." He checked the girth on both saddles and then faced the two men. "Gentlemen, I'm mighty proud of my horseflesh. These mounts are well trained, both to knee and rein commands. If they come back with any hurts, I'll be marking your hides."

Quinton liked a man who took care of his animals. "Rest assured, Mr. Johnson, we'll take good care of these fine ladies."

"Glad to hear it." He removed his hat and wiped his forehead with his shirtsleeve. "How long you plan to keep 'um out?"

"Probably most of the day." Quinton hooked his shoe in the stirrup and mounted the horse. These western saddles would take some getting used to. He wiggled his butt around to become comfortable and patted the mare's neck. "What's her name?"

Johnson rubbed the animal's forelock and smiled. "This here is Sally, and your friend's mare is Roxy." He plopped his hat back on his head. "Where you guys headed, anyways?"

"We're scoping out land for sale in the area. Do you know of any?"

Brian cast him a shocked expression.

"Can't say as I do, but ask over to the mercantile. Herman Kruger knows most of what goes on around here."

"We'll have your animals back by nightfall, if not earlier. We're staying at Mrs. Arbuckle's."

Johnson grinned. "You don't say?" The man was still smirking as they trotted the horses across the street to the store.

An attractive young woman, a basket over her arm, left the mercantile as they approached. Brian, ever the philanderer, removed his hat and bowed in the saddle. "Good day, miss."

Her eyes widened, and she smiled and nodded but didn't speak as she walked down the street, kicking up dust with each step.

They dismounted and tied the reins to the hitching post. Given the darkness inside, it took their eyes a moment to adjust, but the smells of pickles, cigars, and stick candy assailed their senses.

A large man wearing a cloth apron appeared behind the counter. "What can I do for you gents?"

Brian turned on his charm. "We're looking for—"

Quinton elbowed him out of the way. "Land in the area to buy."

"Is that so?"

Brian finally took the hint. "Yes, yes, that's correct."

The man offered his hand. "I'm Herman Kruger. Me and my wife own the store, and most information comes through here at one time or another."

Quinton tipped his hat. He'd seen other men in the West do so as a sign of respect. "I'm Quinton Lynch, and my friend here is Brian MacAuley."

"Where're you gents from?"

"From Ireland, but we hope to become Texas citizens in the near future."

The storekeeper scratched his chin. "Can't say as I rightly know of any place for sale."

"Well, that is a shame." Brian shook his head. "Quinton's daughter married a doctor close to town. He wanted to surprise her by buying a place and settling nearby." He clasped Quinton on the shoulder. "Sorry, old friend. I guess we came to the wrong place."

"Our doc did come home from Boston with a wife, but she's not Irish." He scratched his head. "Think she's German...or maybe it was Swedish."

Quinton held his breath in hopes their discussion would end. Mr. Kruger could be lying, but if so, he'd been pre-warned.

"Thanks for your time, Mr. Kruger."

"Sorry I couldn't help you."

The bright glare of the sun blinded Quinton as they stepped out the door. "We might be wise to invest in one of those wide-brimmed cowboy hats."

Brian snorted. "It's always wise, in your opinion, when we're spending my money."

"A little more sunburn and you might change your tune."

MacAuley touched his face and winced. "You might be right, but for now, let's check out the town. It's so small, it won't take long."

Two buildings stood out—what Quinton assumed was the courthouse and the other that appeared to be a Catholic church. Both buildings were relatively new and added permanence to the town. As they reached the courthouse, the young woman they'd seen at the mercantile walked down the stone steps and into their path. They pulled up. Quinton couldn't imagine what she had to say to them.

"Are you men looking for Aileen?"

****

Aileen hugged Sam's waist as he pulled her close for a kiss. "I'll be back before dark…if the boy's arm is not too hard to set."

"Poor tyke. He's so young."

"Sweetheart, kids are going to climb trees, jump from wagons, any number of activities that can lead to broken bones."

"I know, but I hope Tad waits a long time before we have to face that issue."

"Me too." He released her, turned her around, and swatted her on the rear.

"Hey, you, that hurt!"

Grinning like one of those mules in the barn, he quipped, "Want me to kiss it?"

"Samuel Walker! What are you thinking?" She glanced around. "Tad could have heard you."

"Nah, I looked around first."

She sputtered and spewed, but before she could come up with a rebuttal, he was on his horse and galloping toward town.

Later in the day, Aileen grinned at the memory of Sam's antics as she dusted the living area.

"*Señora.*" Rosa stood in the entryway to the living area. "Two men approach the house. You want I should call Miguel?"

Aileen looked out the window to see her father and Brian MacAuley on horses trotting into the yard. "Yes, please do. Is there a signal to come armed?"

"Yes, indeed, *Señora*. My Miguel will take care of the situation." She hurried off, and Aileen heard the bell ring three times with a short interval in between.

"What about Tad?" Aileen called as she ran into the bedroom and retrieved her pistol out of her night table drawer. She stored it in the pocket of her skirt.

"He knows what to do. He'll hide in the hayloft until Miguel brings him down."

Heart racing, Aileen opened the door and stepped outside. Her father beamed, seemingly glad to see her. And drat it all, she couldn't help but return his smile.

He quickly dismounted and rushed toward her. Appearing out of nowhere, Miguel stepped between them.

With his back to her, shotgun across his arm, he faced her father and asked, "*Señora*, do you wish to see this man?"

Color rose in Quinton's face. "How dare you? I'm her father."

"*Señor* Walker gave strict orders to keep you both" —he nodded toward Mr. MacAuley—"away from the *señora.*"

MacAuley sneered. "No Mexican is going to tell me what I can and cannot do." He started to dismount. The foreman raised the gun and stood ready to fire the weapon.

"Shoot him, Miguel, if either foot leaves the stirrups. Please try to miss the horse, as she is a beautiful animal."

The odious man's mouth dropped open, and he gaped.

"This is a tough land, Mr. MacAuley, and one must adjust to the ways of the West. You are not welcome here. My father is, for a brief time. You can ride on back to town or wait here in the sun. He won't be long. Makes me no difference."

Her father left a short while later, a broken man. Since she'd last seen him, he'd aged ten years. His wrinkled clothes hung on his frame. Aileen stood at the window as he mounted his horse and rode away. Then she allowed the tears to flow.

****

After Miguel filled him in on the day's visitors, Sam clapped him on the back. "Thank you for being here, my friend."

"Pa, Pa, did you know I gots a grandpa?"

"Yes, I do, son."

"How come I didn't get to meet him?" His chin quivered. Sam picked him up and hugged him close. "Don't he like me?"

"He'd love to meet you, but he hurt your mam, and she doesn't want him around her or her family right now, especially you."

"Why?"

"She's afraid he might upset you." He shook his head. "No, it's the other man she fears. Her father owes him a lot of money, and Mr. MacAuley will do anything he can to get the money from your mam."

"Why don't she just give it to him?"

"Because it's not right." Sam set Tad on his feet just outside the door. "I'll explain it all to you later. Let's go in and see how she's doing."

"Her nose is red, and her eyes are all watery. She don't look so good right now."

Sam burst out in a loud guffaw. "Don't tell her that. It'll injure her feelings."

The boy's eyes widened. "Oh…right, Pa. I'll tell her she's real purty."

"Let me talk to her a while. You feed Bandit and take him out for a little walk."

"The *señora* is lying down, Doctor Sam." Rosa shook her head. "Her papa needs a bullwhip to touch his hide."

Aileen smiled as he came into the room. He pulled off his boots, lay down beside her, and slipped his arm under her head. She rolled toward him. "Pretty ugly situation, huh?"

She nodded but didn't speak for a minute. "I feel so guilty. Why don't I just give him the money?"

"You can do so if you want, but you do know your father can stay in the States, and I doubt there is anyway MacAuley could collect, here."

"I told him he could stay in Texas…that we'd help him settle here."

"Sweetheart, the money is yours. If you want to give it to him, do so, but think about what he'll do after he returns to Ireland."

"You're right. He'll build up debt all over again." She bolted up in bed. "Or we could ask Mr. Jamison to pay off MacAuley out of my funds there. Then if he doled out Da's allowance monthly instead of yearly, Da wouldn't have large sums to fritter away."

"That's an excellent idea." She put her head on his chest and snuggled close. "Did he say where he is staying?"

"At Mrs. Arbuckle's."

"We'll ride in to visit him tomorrow." He wondered how they'd learned where Aileen lived. "Did he say how they found you?"

"Mr. Kruger told them your new wife was German and sent them away, but Da said a young woman with long dark hair told them how to get here."

"Ruth."

"Yes, Ruth. I have an odd feeling that Ruth and I will be crossing paths again real soon."

Chapter Eighteen

Sam left Aileen in the buckboard while he walked
up to knock on Mrs. Arbuckle's door. They'd left Tad
at the mercantile to help Martha and Herman. Although
his help was more like talking their ear off, they loved
having him around. Sam knocked on the door and
stepped back as the elderly woman yanked the door
open.

"Oh, it's you, Dr. Walker. Thought it was one of
them no-accounts them foreigners had calling here
yesterday."

"Do you know what they wanted?"

"Oh, yeah, they's wantin' that smooth-tongued
fella to play cards across at the saloon."

"Is he there now?"

"Shore is. The other fella, Mr. Lynch, he's been
sittin' in the parlor staring at the wall all morning.
Came home mighty upset yesterday afternoon."

"Mr. Lynch is my wife's father. Could we come in
and speak with him?"

She stretched her neck to see around him. "Her
father, huh?"

"Yes, ma'am."

"Well, bring her in. Maybe she can make her pa
feel better."

He helped Aileen down from the wagon and
escorted her to the front door. Mrs. Arbuckle studied

Aileen, no doubt taking note of her person from her head to her toes. "Aileen, this is Mrs. Arbuckle, a longstanding citizen of our community and the owner of this boarding house."

"'Tis an honor to meet you, Mrs. Arbuckle."

The woman preened under Sam's heap of praise and took Aileen's hand to lead her inside. "A pleasure, young woman." She led them into the parlor, an empty room. "Why, Mr. Lynch must have gone to his room." She waved to the sofa. "Take a seat, and I'll collect him."

A few minutes later, a middle-aged man with graying red hair came into the room. His bleak expression brightened as he saw Aileen. She walked to him, wrapped her arms around his waist, and laid her head against his chest.

He clasped her close and dropped a kiss on top of her head. "Daughter, it's glad I am to see you."

Aileen stepped back and held her hand out to Sam. "Da, this is my husband, Doctor Sam Walker. Sam, my father, Quinton Lynch."

Sam wasn't about to be cordial to her father. He'd tried to sell his own daughter for financial gain. What kind of man could stoop so low? He glanced at Aileen and saw the pleading expression in her eyes. He softened his own countenance and nodded to the man. "Lynch."

No doubt the older man sensed Sam's animosity. "I know you must despise me, Doctor Walker." He shuddered. "I despise myself."

"And well you should, driving your daughter to flee her home country to escape your plotting. To top it all, you forced her into a marriage that neither of us had planned on or wanted."

A soft cry had him whirling to realize the effect of his remark on Aileen. She stood, her fingers covering her trembling lips. He reached out to her, but she shook his arm off and moved to sit on the sofa. "Sweetheart, I didn't mean it like it sounded."

"No matter, Sam. It's been said, and you can't take it back." Her expression bleak, she motioned to her father. "Have a seat, Da."

Sam winced at her choice of words. He'd hurt her…again.

Lynch sat beside her and patted her knee. "Has he no' been good to you, lass? You said yesterday you were very happy."

"Don't worry yourself. I'm deliriously happy."

"But—"

She held up a hand and shook her head. "Sam and I discussed your situation and have come up with a plan." Lynch looked from him to Aileen. "I'll give you the money to pay Mr. MacAuley, but you'll not receive it until you return to Ireland. The money will be waiting for you at Mr. Jamison's law office."

"'Tis shamed I am to accept it, but I have no choice, and I thank you, daughter."

"There is a stipulation. I don't want you getting yourself into the same fix again. To help prevent you from gambling, your yearly income will be paid out in a monthly allowance."

His face reddened. "You intend to treat me like a lad off at university?"

"Yes, Father. You've shown you're not to be trusted with money within easy reach. This way, if you spend your income each month, you'll at least have revenue from the mill and next month's allotment to look forward to."

"I doubt MacAuley will be pleased."

Sam stood. "He doesn't have to be pleased. We'll pay your passage back to Ireland. Cut yourself loose from the man before he drags you down any further."

"Sam's right, Da."

"I know it's the truth."

"I think we better go relieve Herman and Martha. Tad's probably eaten enough candy to be sick by now."

Lynch stood and offered Aileen a hand. "Aileen told me all about the boy. Seems to think he's mighty special."

Sam cleared this throat. Aileen's affection for the boy warmed him in every way. Never in his wildest dreams had he believed a woman could come near to replacing Jane, but Aileen was close. "Tad's crazy about your daughter. Even calls her Mam now."

"You don't say." Lynch clasped Aileen's hand, his smile genuine. "I wish I'd been able to meet the tyke." Aileen started to speak, but he shook his head. "Your reasoning for keeping him away is perfectly understandable. Perhaps we'll see each other another time."

Sam's opinion of the man softened. "Get your affairs in order, Lynch. Then come back and stay a while."

Aileen flashed Sam a grateful smile and leaned into her father's side. "Oh, yes, Da. Please come back as soon as you can." She chuckled. "But make it in the winter months. This summer heat is unbearable."

Lynch tugged on his shirt collar. "Indeed it is."

****

Aileen held Sam's arm as he helped her into the wagon. She settled her skirts around her while Sam released the brake. He flicked the reins and called, "Haw," and the mules made a sharp turn to the left. "Walk on." The animals started walking. It was a short distance to the mercantile, and it seemed they'd no sooner started than they stopped. "Do you want to come in for a minute and visit with Martha?"

"No, I don't think so. I'll just sit here and wait for you." It was difficult for her to be nonchalant and interested in chatting at the moment. Aileen wished her feelings weren't injured so easily, or that she could toss rejoinders back to sooth her pride, but she couldn't. It wasn't in her nature. Just when she thought their happiness might be real and lasting, Sam snatched it back again with a remark like he'd made today.

"To top it all, you forced her into a marriage that neither of us had planned on or wanted."

The words stung. And they wouldn't be easy to forget. Her silence wasn't intentional. In a sense, it was a protective devise. If she broke her reticence right now, she'd probably cry, and she didn't want Tad to see her thus.

"You don't need anything?"

"Nothing I can think of at the moment. Rosa will be coming in for supplies tomorrow. If I think of something, I can add it to her list."

The muscles in Sam's jaw jumped. He was angry, either at himself for his comment or at her for being upset. So be it. "Suit yourself." He jumped down from the wagon and strode into the store. A short moment later he exited, Herman Kruger on his heels bearing a shotgun. He rushed into the saloon next door. Sam handed Aileen a note and then reached under the wagon seat and withdrew his gun and holster. When he'd strapped the Army Colt on, he grabbed his rifle.

"What's wrong, Sam?" She looked around. "Where's Tad?"

"Brian MacAuley has him."

She glanced down at the note. In crisp strokes of the pen, MacAuley had written, "I want the money I'm owed. You'll get the boy back, unharmed, when I acquire the money owed me." She climbed out of the wagon and stood, while Sam, at a lope, ran up the street toward Mrs. Arbuckle's. Moments later, he came out with Quinton. The two rushed toward the stable. She hurried across the street to meet them.

"You're not going, Aileen." He nodded toward the store. "Go stay with Martha."

"I'm going, Sam, either with you or on my own."

"There will be gunfire. You could be wounded. Tad doesn't need to see that happen."

Several men poured from the saloon, mounted their horses, and met them in front of Johnson's Livery. "I can't stay here. I'm going with you or by myself." She clutched at the back of his shirt while he saddled a horse. "How did he get Tad to go with him?"

Sam snorted. "Ruth."

Aileen had known she and Ruth would butt heads again, and today was the day. "Mr. Johnson, I need a horse, also."

"Yes, ma'am." He glanced at Sam. Her husband closed his eyes for a minute and then nodded.

Five minutes later, they were mounted and formed in a circle around Sam. His face was leached of color, and deep lines marred his forehead. Aileen wanted to comfort him but didn't know how. "We believe he's taken Tad to the old Stokley place about a mile south of town. No shooting unless I give the order. I want my boy unhurt, preferably Ruth and MacAuley also, but if it becomes necessary, I'll kill them both."

Aileen pulled her horse next to Sam's. He took her hand and kissed it. Her gaze searched his, and the tenderness in his eyes made her gasp. "Men, look after my wife. My boy doesn't need to lose another mother."

He set his heels into his horse, and the animal shot forward before anyone could respond. At the speed they traveled, they arrived outside the shack in short time. Two horses were tied up out front. The roof had caved in, and the adobe walls crumbled, but it was still easy for MacAuley to keep Tad out of sight.

They all dismounted, and Sam walked toward the ruins. "MacAuley, I want my son. Now."

"Sorry about that, old chap, but you can have him when I get my money."

"Brian, Aileen and her husband visited me this very morning. They're sending a wire to Jamison to hand over the funds when we visit him in Dublin." Da started toward the building from a different angle than Sam. He held out his hands. "Come on, now, give the boy up. He is my grandson, you know."

"You're a fool, Lynch. They're not going to let us just catch a stage and ride out of here."

Da glanced at Sam.

"You've got that right, MacAuley," Sam said. "You'll go to jail, if you don't hang for kidnapping. Of course, if I have my way, I'll put a bullet between your eyes, and we'll not have to worry about a trial."

"You can't do that."

"Watch me. I can do it, and there's not a man here who won't stand behind me. We don't tolerate the abuse of children."

"I've not hurt a hair on the boy's head. Ask sweet Ruth over here."

"Pa, he smacked me." Tad's voice quivered.

"Shut up, kid, before I stick you with this knife."

Aileen walked up to stand by Sam. "Mr. MacAuley, let me trade places with Tad. I'm the one you want."

"Nooo," Sam roared. He caught her shoulder and pushed her behind him.

Brian MacAuley cackled. "Now, that's a deal I'll consider."

"You're not going in there, Aileen. He's too much of a coward to touch Tad, but he has a vendetta against you."

"Trust me, Sam. You've taught me how to defend myself, and I remember all you've shown me." He gazed into her eyes as if searching for answers. He shook his head. "Please, Sam. This is all my fault."

He swung around to Quinton. "Like hell. It's your father's fault."

Lynch hung his head. "He's right, lass. I brought this on you and your family."

"Mr. MacAuley, send Ruth out, and then I'll come in."

"My pleasure. She's served her purpose." They heard a screech from Ruth. "I said get out!"

Ruth stumbled out, lip bleeding and a bruise beginning on her cheek. She fell and landed on her knees not far from Aileen and Sam. Her gaze beseeched them to help her, but neither one moved. Her actions wouldn't be easily forgiven or forgotten. Finally Herman stepped forward, reached down, grabbed her arm, and yanked her up.

"I'll be careful, Sam. And he won't hurt me. Somehow I know it." She covered her heart. "In here." She slipped her arms around his waist, and he held her tightly.

Voice gruff, he whispered in her ear. "I can't lose you, Aileen. You better come back."

"I will."

Aileen walked toward the gaping hole that had once been a doorway. "I'm coming in, MacAuley."

When she stepped inside, he leered at her. He held Tad by the neck of his shirt. She ignored his crudity. "Let him go now. I promise not to move."

He released Tad, and the boy ran to her and wrapped his arms around her waist. "I knew you and Pa would find me."

She dropped a kiss to the top of his head. "Always, dear boy. Always." She stepped back from him and pushed him toward the door. "Go on to your pa now. I'll be all right." He ran, and Sam lifted him in his arms. Herman stepped forward, took him, and stepped away.

"Well, well, well. Never thought I'd have you at my mercy like this." He reached out with the knife and placed the end under her chin. She lifted her head. "You are one beautiful—"

A shot sounded. Blood and brain matter splashed against her face and clothes. The world blurred, and…

Chapter Nineteen

A hoarse cry burst in his chest and escaped through his lips as he barreled into the adobe ruin. A gory sight welcomed him. He dropped to the floor beside Aileen. She lay in a heap, covered in bloody gore. He ran his hands over her body, looking for wounds. Air rushed from his lungs when he found none. *Thank you, God.* He lifted her in trembling arms and held her to his chest. Tears burned his eyes, and he struggled to keep them from falling.

He stood and carried her out without a backward glance at what was left of MacAuley. The man's shattered skull was a sight he didn't want Aileen or Tad to view. Men parted as he carried Aileen out. Someone spread a blanket under a scrub oak, and he laid her down. "I need some water."

A cowboy whose name he didn't recall handed him a canteen. Another offered him a clean bandana. He set to cleaning as much of the gore off Aileen as he could. He didn't want her to wake and find it all over her. Wasn't much he could do about the dress. A good wiping with the wet rag might help. He turned to catch sight of several men tying MacAuley's body, wrapped in a blanket, to a horse.

Lynch hovered at his side. "Is she unhurt?"

"Yes, but she's in shock. Seeing MacAuley's head explode must have been more than her mind could grasp." He felt for the gun Aileen carried in her pocket. It was there, but cool to the touch. She hadn't killed the man.

He looked up and around at the men standing in groups, talking. One man stood apart, a man who looked familiar, though he knew he'd never seen him before. A Winchester rifle lay across his arm. His eyes, the same color as Aileen's, never left her face. The man was the one pictured in Aileen's locket—her natural father—Joseph Chamberlain. As if sensing Sam's gaze, his own flicked up to meet Sam's. He nodded.

Sam motioned him over and stood to greet the man. "Captain Chamberlain, I can't thank you enough for your actions today."

They shook hands. "I wish it could have been prevented, and I'm grateful my father taught me to be a dead shot." He squatted and looked closely at Aileen. With two fingers, he stroked her cheek and brushed hair back from her forehead. "I've not seen her before." He brushed at a tear that leaked from his eye. "She's beautiful. Just like her mother, the love of my life." He stood, faced Sam, and continued, "How do you know my name?"

"From Aileen. I've seen the locket and the uncanny resemblance between father and daughter is hard to miss."

Chamberlain smiled. "I'd have given anything to take my rightful place, with her mother as my bride, to be a father to our child."

Then he turned to Quinton and offered his hand. "Mr. Lynch. I know until recently you've been a good father to Aileen. I'm grateful, and wish by all the stars above I could have returned in time to claim her."

"She's a delightful young woman…the joy of my life." Quinton shook his head. "I'm ashamed of me actions these past few years."

"None of us is perfect. Perhaps after today all will be better."

****

Aileen woke for the second time in bed, dressed in a clean gown. When they'd arrived home, Sam had stripped her and lowered her into a warm bath. He'd shampooed her hair and washed her with lilac-scented soap that Rosa found somewhere. She'd been too weak and tired to argue when he'd wrapped her hair in a towel, slipped a clean white gown over her head, and carried her to their bedroom.

Tad lay curled up at her side, asleep. She turned to face him and gently pushed the hair back from his sweaty forehead. He opened his eyes and smiled. Then he lurched out of bed and ran for the door. "Pa, she's awake."

Before she could object, the room filled with people—Sam, Rosa, Miguel, Da, and a man she'd never met but knew by the tingles of her scalp was the man pictured in her locket. Unable to hold her stress in any longer, she covered her face and burst into sobs.

Sam sat on the bed and cradled her close. "It's all right, sweetheart. You need a good cry."

She sniffed. "But I feel so stupid."

"You shouldn't. You've been a brave woman. It's only natural that your body give in to the stress and release some of those emotions."

"Thank you all for caring for me."

Rosa patted her arm. "We love you, *Señora*. Rest, and call if you need anything." She left, taking Miguel with her.

Da kissed her forehead. "I'll leave also. There's someone here who's come a long way to meet you."

He left the room, and Sam followed and closed the door. She turned to the man who her mother had loved so deeply—her natural father. At a loss for what to do, she went with instinct and held out her arms.

****

The house was quiet. The captain was in the guest room, and Quinton had returned to Mrs. Arbuckle's. Sam and Aileen lay in bed facing each other. He tucked her close and smoothed his hand over her hip. "Have you ever fainted before?"

She pulled back and studied his face. "No, never. Why do you ask?"

"Hmm, just wondering."

"It was probably the stress and shock of seeing that horrid man's head explode…" She shuddered. "It'll be hard to wash that memory from my mind."

"Possibly. When were your last monthly courses?" Like he didn't know. He was as in tune with her body as he was with his own. He struggled with the truth. He didn't want to spoil her happiness, but having a baby was a nightmare for him. She could die in childbirth…their child could also die. Though she knew about his fears, he'd do his best to bury them for now.

"Why…I'm not sure." She stared into space a minute, and then widened her eyes. "I'm almost two weeks late."

"I think you're expecting, sweetheart." He could feel the rapid beat of her heart against his chest.

"Expecting a…a baby?"

With his finger, he traced a line from her forehead

down her nose to touch her lips. "Yes, a baby. You have all the symptoms." He palmed a breast. "Fuller and more tender breasts, missing a cycle, and then the fainting this morning. Yes, I'd say you're definitely pregnant."

She sobbed against his neck. "A baby. We're having a baby."

He patted her back and made soothing sounds while his mind spun in circles.

Her body stilled. "I'm sorry, Sam. I know you don't want more children, but I'm thrilled."

"I'd love more children, but I fear for you. I don't want to lose you, Aileen." He twisted his hand in the hair at the base of her neck and tugged her head back to look into her face. "I love you, sweetheart. Lord knows I didn't want to, but you gave me no choice in the matter." He brushed the side of her face with his lips. "I'll shrivel up and die if I lose you."

Doubt and confusion clouded her features. "Do you mean it...really?"

He brushed the tears from her cheeks and kissed her trembling lips. "Yes, my love, I mean it. I've loved you for a good while but wasn't ready to admit my feelings. Today when you traded places with Tad, I couldn't deny my feelings any longer." He chuckled at the memory. "You pretty well cinched my affections when you punched Ruth. I knew then I'd married a woman who'd fight for those she loved and what she held dear."

"Ruth... You might know she'd get out of town before I got to smack her again."

****

Aileen couldn't contain her excitement at breakfast

the next day. She wanted to share their news with everyone, but Sam didn't want Tad to know just yet. "The boy will be asking every day when his sister or brother will arrive."

Da had ridden in from town in time for breakfast and would spend the day. Tad was beside himself when he learned he had two grandpas. It pleased Aileen to see the men pay attention to the boy. He begged them to come outside to watch Bandit in action. Sam spoke up. "Go on out and help Miguel. We need another cup of coffee, but we'll be along soon." As soon as he headed out to play with Bandit, Sam nodded for her to go ahead.

"We're going to have a baby."

Congratulations were shared, and cups of coffee used to toast the coming of a healthy child. Aileen touched her belly often, in awe to think a new life grew within. Da turned weepy. No doubt he missed Mam and was reminded of how happy she'd have been to learn she'd be a grandmother.

Evidently, while she'd been asleep the day before, Da and Papa, the name she'd settled on to call the captain, became more acquainted and had decided to travel to Boston together. The stage would leave the following afternoon. Ruth had left town yesterday. She'd been given a choice of leaving town or facing kidnapping charges.

"I wish you both didn't have to leave so soon."

"Aye, that's me wish also, daughter, but I must take the news of MacAuley's passing to his family and settle my debt. I'm sure Mr. Jamison will be a great help."

"And I must return home to my wife. Though she

198

understood my need to come to Texas to meet you, she'll not be happy if I stay away from the children too long." Yesterday he'd shared the story of his life upon returning to Boston without Mam. After several years he'd married, and they had three children, all below the age of fifteen.

"I hope you'll come back after the baby is born and bring your family. You too, Da." She smiled at Sam. "Do you think we could build on a couple more rooms?"

He chuckled. "I think we can manage that. As soon as the crops are in this fall, and when the stock don't need tending, Miguel and I'll get started."

The captain sat to her left at the table. He lifted his pocket watch, with the portrait of him and her mother, from his pocket and placed it in her hand. "I want you to save this for your first son."

"Are you sure you want to part with it?"

"I'm sure. Doing so will make my wife happy. My keeping it has always been a point of contention with her, plus you have your mother's locket to pass on to your first daughter." He turned to Sam. "I expect you have something of your father's to hand down to Tad. I hope you won't take this gift as a slight to him."

"Never. And yes, I have my father's gold pocket watch." He chuckled. "Tad admires it often."

"He's a fine boy, but Quinton, if we want to stay in the lad's good graces, we'd better hustle out and meet this Bandit of his."

****

Several months after her father arrived in Ireland, Aileen received a letter from him. She'd read it many times, the paper wrinkled in places from being in her pocket. She flattened the sheet against the desktop and read again: *Mr. Jamison said that MacAuley hadn't filed my debt with the courts, and he could find no living relatives, thus my debt is no longer. Though relieved I won't be using your money, I feel badly at the man's demise and can't but feel his death wouldn't have occurred if I'd not gambled with him.*

Aileen was proud Da admitted and understood his culpability in the situation. Hopefully he'd learned his lesson and would run the mill and be happy. She lifted a sheet of paper from the drawer and dipped the nib of the pen in the inkwell.

Dear Da,

I'm so pleased you're doing well. I received the baby things you had Mattie box up and send. I just know this little one is a girl, so they're perfect. Tell Mattie I love her, and hello to Charles, Lucy, and Mabel.

Rosa stuck her head in the door. "How about a cup of tea, *Señora*?"

"I'd love one." She stood. "I'll come in and sit at the table. Please join me, and let's use the Irish teacups." Rosa's pregnancy was far along. The sickness had passed, and other than getting big and carrying the extra weight, she was as cheerful as ever. Fortunately for Aileen, so far she hadn't been sick. Hopefully she wouldn't.

Sam and Miguel stayed busy building a room on to Rosa and Miguel's house. They were almost finished and would soon start adding on to the main house. The sound of hammers hitting nails didn't bother her. It meant her life was growing and changing, just as her body was. Aileen smiled over her cup. She'd never been happier with her life than in this dry, barren land. It was so different from what she'd been accustomed to in Ireland.

Oh, on occasion she missed the green hills, but they'd spend a day at the springs having a picnic, and her longing would ease.

Rosa jumped, sloshing her tea. It spilled over into her saucer. She grabbed her belly.

Aileen set her tea down and rushed around the table. "Are you in pain?"

The young woman laughed. "Oh, no. This little one just kicked." She took Aileen's hand and placed it on the spot. The child moved again, actually pushing Rosa's belly out. Aileen could feel its little foot.

"'Tis amazing." She placed her hand over her own growing child. How much longer before she felt movement?

As if reading her mind, Rosa squeezed her hand. "It will be soon, *Señora*."

****

Sam wiped the sweat from his brow and took a dipperful of water from the wooden bucket on the bed of the wagon. He drank a cupful and then poured a little on top of his head. It was early May, and as usual the temperatures soared. The addition was coming along nicely and would be ready for their guests when they arrived in September. Each bedroom would have French doors onto the patio. How they'd manage with six extra people in the house, plus the baby, he didn't know. Aileen was thrilled, so he'd not complain.

He'd just plopped his hat back on his head and picked up his hammer when someone rang the bell. His heart jumped into his throat. Aileen was going into labor! He struggled to calm himself before facing his wife. It wouldn't do for her to see his fear and concern. *Have faith, Sam.* He dropped his head. *Please, God, let Aileen have a safe delivery and a healthy baby.*

Rosa met him in the kitchen. "The *señora*'s water has broken, and her pains have started. Miguel has gone for Mrs. Mendoza to help you with the delivery."

"Thank you, Rosa. Bring her on in when she arrives. Will you take Tad home with you and Miguel?"

"*Si*, we'd be happy to have the boy." She lifted her baby from the cradle kept in the dining area. "I'll give Miguel the news."

"Thank you, Rosa. I'll come get Tad in the morning."

"No need. We will bring him when we come."

"Sam." Aileen's clear voice didn't sound in the least distressed.

He met her at the door of their bedroom. In her long white nightgown, she appeared angelic, her smile as radiant as an angel's halo. He enfolded her in his arms, their child between them preventing close contact. "Oh, Sam, I'm so excited."

"Me too, sweetheart." He kissed the tip of her nose. "Come along now, let's tuck you into the bed."

Eight hours later, Maureen Olivia Walker, screaming her little head off, slipped from Aileen's body into his waiting hands. Tears blurred Sam's vision as he raised the infant so Aileen could see. "Our daughter." He chuckled. "I think she has your temper."

Aileen laughed. "Oh, I hope so."

He laid the infant in the outstretched blanket Mrs. Mendoza held, then cut the umbilical cord and tied it off. Sam stood. "Let me take her, Mrs. Mendoza." He carried her to the washbasin for her first bath. "I'll clean her up and give her a quick checkup."

The older woman nodded. "I'll deliver the afterbirth and bathe the missus."

"Let me know if there is anything to be concerned about."

"Now, Dr. Walker, this young woman is perfectly healthy. She's had an easy delivery. You stop worrying, and clean that baby up so her mama can feed her before she starves to death."

"Yes, ma'am." She was right. With the infant still crying her displeasure, he carefully immersed her in the warm water and talked to her as he washed the waxy coating from her skin and hair. "Welcome to our home, daughter. Now, I know I'll be putty in your hands, so please, be easy on me. I don't know much about girls." Her cries lessened and then stopped. She stared up at him with her big blue eyes. The little minx wasn't an hour old, and she'd already stolen his heart.

He laid the clean and diapered baby in Aileen's arms. "Ach, she's beautiful, Sam. Look at those beautiful blue eyes, just like Mam's." She sniffed and wiped a tear off her cheek. "Maureen is a big name for such a small bundle. How would you feel about calling her Mauri?"

"I like it very much."

Maureen threw out her fists and started to fuss again. "I think she's hungry."

Sam kicked off his shoes and crawled onto the bed. Propped up on one arm, he watched as his daughter nursed greedily.

Aileen smiled up at him. "I love you, Sam. When we boarded the train in Boston, I never dreamed I'd be this happy."

"Aw, sweetheart, and I you." He leaned in and kissed her lips. "Your love and courage have made me a better man and healed scars I thought would never close."

The kitchen door slammed, and they heard Tad thundering through the house. He appeared at their bedroom door, Bandit at his heels. He turned to the dog and said, "Stay."

Bandit hit his haunches and didn't move. Tad tiptoed to the bed. It was funny to watch, after his loud entrance. He leaned over and peered at the baby. "Mam, Rosa said I gots a baby sister. I'd rather have a brother. Can we trade her?"

Sam had to bite his lip to keep from laughing. Mauri popped her eyes open, gazed straight at Tad, and waved her fists. *Oh, boy, she's getting ready to demand her breakfast.*

Tad studied her for a few minutes. "Well, she's kinda purty. I guess we can keep her."

A word about the author...

Linda LaRoque is a Texas girl, but the first time she got on a horse, it tossed her in the road, dislocating her right shoulder. Forty years passed before she got on another, but it was older, slower, and she was wiser. Plus, her students looked on, and it was important to save face.

A retired teacher who loves West Texas, its flora and fauna, and its people, Linda's stories paint pictures of life, love, and learning set against the raw landscape of ranches and rural communities in Texas and the Midwest. She is a member of RWA, her local chapter of HOTRWA, NTRWA, and Texas Mountain Trail Writers.

Linda writes contemporary western romances, time travel romances, futuristic romances, and women's fiction.

Visit Linda at these locations.

http://www.lindalaroqueauthor.blogspot.com

www.lindalaroque.com

https://www.facebook.com/linda.laroque

https://www.facebook.com/Author-Linda-LaRoque-119422624783798/timeline/

https://twitter.com/LindaLaRoque

http://www.goodreads.com/author/show/649259.Linda_LaRoque

Linda's Amazon Page